PHANTOM MASQUERADE

A. L. HAWKE

PHANTOM HEART, LLC

ISBN: 9781953919557

ISBN: 9781953919564 (ebook)

ISBN: 978-1-953919-54-0 (hardcover)

Library of Congress Control Number: 2021944755

Line edited by Stephanie Ward

Proofread by Faith Williams

Cover Design © 2021 by Mirella Santana

www.mirellasantana.com.br

Published by Phantom Heart, LLC

27702 Crown Valley Pkwy, Suite D4, #201

Ladera Ranch, CA 92694

Printed and bound in the United States of America

First printing September, 2021

Learn more about A.L. Hawke at www.alhawke.com

Correspondence: contact@alhawke.com

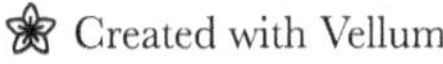 Created with Vellum

THE HARLEQUIN

A fire truck of laughing clowns with squeaky horns, dangling over a red-and-white striped engine, rushed from the left side of the auditorium toward center stage. Behind came the lion trainer, slashing the air with his whip near an empty diamond-studded cage. And acrobats in striped tights jumped and tumbled beside the fire truck, up and down, doing somersaults and flips, with jugglers not far behind. Then music: a disturbing mix of puissant class with the frenzied Big Top. An orchestra triumphant thundering *Don Giovanni* in D minor. Then light shone down on raspberry lips and the white-and-black painted face of the Don Juan himself.

Mina leaned forward, captivated. She recognized this clown. This was Monsieur Antonio Vollini, her teacher and close friend back in the university in Paris. An older man with a dark beard and thick black eyebrows. A vibrant man, now thrusting his hands high, wearing a bright-red flannel suit with a tail and a sad painted smile. His face was powdered paler than the fools around him, yet he walked across the stage, emitting grandeur. The sight of him bordered between ridiculous and brilliant—exactly like his play. Exactly like him. Antonio Vollini. The harlequin.

He stiffened his body and held his head high, demanding attention. And she was close enough to the stage to see a smile behind the painted frown. Then he waved his hand in broad strokes before the audience and bowed, seemingly adoring the adulation as the crowd applauded. But when she turned and looked behind her, there was no one there. The seats of the auditorium were empty.

The harlequin removed his red coat and spun the cloth around like a magician, and pigeons flew out from within the satin folds. Then the clown gave another majestic bow, throwing his coat to the crowd amidst thunderous applause— from no one.

"This is my favorite part," whispered a male voice.

Mina was surprised to see a man sitting beside her, wearing a shiny black mask covering one eye and much of his face. This stranger touched her fingers with soft white gloves, which contrasted with his pitch-black mask. As she gazed at him, trying to recollect who he was, he leaned forward in his seat, just as enthralled as she was. The open part of his mask revealed a goatee and stubble extending up his hard cheek-bone. It made for a handsome portrait. Then she felt tingles as he pressed her fingers again with those soft cotton gloves. She followed his muscular arm and chest in a sleeveless tuxedo up to his broad shoulders. He turned and flashed a smile, looking at her with bright jade eyes, rubbing her fingers some more.

"Enjoying the play?" he asked.

She recognized a French accent.

"Yes." *Who are you?*

The crash of drums jerked her eyes back to the perform-ers. Two women wearing tall, frilly hats and white tights rode on tall bicycles—penny-farthings—to center stage. They circled the Harlequin and jumped off, swaying and contorting around him. Their white spandex pants and thin shirts twisted over their shapely hips and chests. Then a third ballet dancer interrupted the dance, rushing to the clown. She kissed his white-painted cheek, running her fingers along his beard and gliding them over his chest and stomach. She touched his shoulder then grabbed him, swaying and dancing to Mozart. And the Harlequin, in his ridiculous flabby white pants, twirled in a senseless bourrée.

The sound of a trumpet, an odd, shrill instrument in the midst of such lovely strings and choral music, broke the spell. Lights dimmed. The music stopped. There was a roar of applause—from no one.

When a yellow floodlight lit the stage once more, two tall steel towers rose until they nearly touched the ceiling; a tightrope stretched between them. To Mina's right, the Harlequin sat very high atop one of the towers on a narrow pedestal. It grew dark, with only an array of rainbow light shining over him. He shifted his balance and, for a moment, it looked like he was going to fall. There were gasps. He threw up a white-gloved index finger. His hand seemed to be in step with the orchestra. One solitary finger. He dropped it and raised it again, miming a conductor's movement, as if he were conducting a great symphony with the colored lights. A few onlookers in empty seats laughed.

Then the strangest of strange things happened. Although the Harlequin was painted in clown face, wearing baggy pants and ridiculous circus shoes, and at times swayed stupidly as if about to fall from the rafter, he sang a baritone accompaniment to Mozart. He sang and the circus transformed into an opera. Although his huge red clown shoes were barely balancing atop the narrow platform, he was absorbed by the music, looking into the bright light as his voice bellowed.

Mina recognized the song as the second and final act of *Don Giovanni*, playing again. There Toni stood, high above Mina, with his lovely baritone voice, singing his best Italian. She mouthed the words as if accompanying him. Back at the Conservatoire de Paris, they had sung this opera together. The orchestra thundered and, as he sang, she no longer thought of music. She thought of him. Toni. Her harlequin. Her clown. Her dear friend. But he seemed sad, with his painted frown, singing to her. He looked right down at her, only her, for there was no one else in the auditorium … except the stranger.

"Enjoying it?" the stranger asked again.

She nodded and pulled her fingers away from the stranger's soft glove to wipe a tear running down her cheek. The orchestra finally rang in a crescendo.

And here is where I fell.

Toni cried out a shrill scream of terror, so unsettling and discordant from such a jovial man. The shriek shook her. She felt dizzy. Everything spun and grew dark.

When she opened her eyes, a flood of bright red and purple and green began shining up from below. Now she was atop the high precipice, naked, looking down over her chest and shaky legs. She adjusted her bare feet, trying to balance on the cold, narrow steel ledge, in the same place Toni had been standing, singing his opera. She had replaced him. The light brightened, nearly blinding her. She could barely balance.

And here is where I fall.

MACARONI AND CHEESE ON BROADWAY

Mina sat in a large booth by her lonesome, waiting for Toni, in a swanky downtown Manhattan restaurant. It was an elegant establishment, lined with windows, with white-columned walls and waiters wearing formal suits. Really swank. A single candle flickered on the center of her table. And quaint. Her booth was surrounded by a three-walled window overlooking the bright lights of the New York City skyline. The city was absolutely breathtaking. But she was high—too high—over fifty floors up. The street was so far below her.

She spotted Toni. He approached the maître d' and bound inside. He wore an elegant black suit. His short black hair and thick beard were perfectly manicured, and his skin was a bit tanned. The only major imperfection was his nose. It was a little round and ruddy, perfect for reminding her of the clown in her dream. She was surprised at how little he had changed.

She stood up and embraced him as he kissed her cheek.

"Oh, Mina, cara mia … cara Mina, you're so lovely." He had a thick Italian accent. "Absolutely lovely. I'm so happy to see you."

"Me too, Toni. Hi."

"Sorry I'm late but, believe it or not, it had to do with our play."

"*Our* play?" she asked with a chuckle.

"Si. You look breathtaking. Stunning."

"Thanks. It's great to see you too. You look pretty good yourself."

"Time moves fast, eh?" He removed his suit jacket, draping it over a seat across from her at the table. Then he sat down with her and looked outside the window, taking a deep breath as if enjoying the fragrance of the view.

"Quite a nice table you arranged," she said with some smugness.

"Meeting with you, my dear…" He gestured with a swoop of his hand. "I planned the best. The very best." He smiled again.

She loved his smile, but his broad hand gesture disturbed her a little, reminding her of her dream.

He shrugged and stared into her eyes for a moment—just stared. Then he looked some more.

"What?" she asked with a nervous laugh. "What is it?"

"Bellissima." He shook his head. "Simply bellissima. Did you order anything yet?"

"No. It's so great seeing you. And thanks for the invitation. This place is amazing."

It really was. She looked up from the menu, under the candlelight, and admired the view again. Then she laughed as he tapped his fingers on the table, thumbing through the menu as if it was a bother.

After brushing through a couple of pages, he put it down. "How are you, Mina? Tell me. I mean, how are you *really*?"

"What do you mean?"

"Not just hello. How are you? Are you still living at the university? That's what you said on the phone. Painting? You have so many talents. I introduced you to Blateman when you first arrived in New York. Did he help display your artwork?"

"No. He … well, it just didn't work out."

"Dancing then?" He leaned back in the chair, stroking his beard.

A waiter in a double-breasted navy-blue suit came back with two glasses and a bottle of wine before she could respond.

"What's this?" Mina asked.

"Celebration," Toni said with a smile and a wink. "For you."

"Celebrating what?"

"*You.*"

The waiter uncorked the bottle and presented the cork to Toni to sniff, then offered it to Mina. She waited until both glasses were poured by the waiter and he left.

"I'm doing fine," Mina said. "Thank you, Toni."

"That makes me so happy." He raised his glass. "To you and I, my dear. And the past. I've missed you so. Your voice is exquisite, but it is not as welcoming as the vision of your soul."

"Oh Toni, you still talk silly."

"Arabesque?" he asked, laughing with her. "True, true." He stared at his wine glass. "I like to have fun."

"You *are* fun."

He raised his glass to that. Then he cocked his head and looked at her curiously. "You remember before, no? Remember what I said right before you left Paris with that gentleman you were with? I can't remember his name."

"It didn't work out between us."

"You told me. But do you remember what I offered you?"

Yes. She remembered. Toni had offered her a job. She hoped that's what he was proposing tonight, and that's why she had spent so long fixing her hair, applying the perfect makeup, and putting on an attractive, but professional, navy-blue dress in her apartment. She had chosen her finest clothes. Even around her neck, she'd added her favorite diamond stud silver necklace. The diamond was tiny, but the chain was her best silver.

"I sent you my screenplay," he added. "Did you read it?"

"For sure." After all, it had imprinted itself in her dream.

"What did you think?"

A black shadow brushed by the window and drew shade over their table. At first, she mistook it for a bird, but then she realized that was impossible in the middle of the night. Toni still stared at her, waiting for her to respond.

She looked outside and jumped. A black figure in a cape stood like a perched raven with hands tucked in coat pockets and head tilted downward. Although the man gazed down, he wore a mask—the same half-mask that the figure in her dream had worn. He seemed very real, only he stood midair and she could see two buildings through him.

The waiter returned.

Mina forced a fake smile at the waiter. Toni glanced at the window a couple of times and then just furrowed his brow. The waiter had placed a salad plate before each of them and a basket of bread. Mina quickly grabbed her fork and stuck it into a carrot. Her hand shook as she brought it to her mouth.

"Are you all right?" Toni asked.

"Um-hmm." *Get it together, Mina. Not now.*

"So … what did you think?" he asked again.

She took a deep breath, squeezed her hand under the table tight, and closed her eyes for a second.

"Hmm? What'd I think about what?"

"My musical, Mina? Did you like it?"

"Uh-huh."

She dipped another carrot in the dressing and tasted it. It was sweet and tart—absolutely delicious. She savored every bite.

"Umm," she said. "This food is really good."

Toni raised his eyebrow, staring impatiently, waiting for her response.

"Oh, Toni, well … it was different. But yes, it was good.

All your stuff is really good." She swallowed some kale and finally summoned enough courage to glance back at the window. The apparition was gone.

"It will be the number-one show on Broadway. *If* you help me. Remember what I offered you before you left? That offer is still good, now on Broadway. What do you say?"

"Well, well, well. But I haven't danced in a long time. Not since we lived in Paris."

He just smiled.

"A show on Broadway?" she asked.

"Si." He folded his arms.

Mina swirled more leaves into her salad dressing, enjoying whatever heavenly stuff it was. The food was so good. It was a pleasant distraction from the window.

Toni looked at her with a warm smile.

She stabbed some more leaves and crunched on them, patting her chin with her cloth napkin surreptitiously to make sure the dressing remained inside her mouth and not on her lips. She laughed inwardly as he just attacked his plate, seeming not to care about his appearance or the food. It was cute.

"Why Mozart?" she asked.

"Che?" he replied with his mouth full.

"Why Mozart, Toni? I don't get it. I never did."

"I love Mozart."

"I do too. But why did you stick him in a play about clowns?"

"The play is an adaptation of *Don Juan.*"

"I know."

"Don Juan was in Mozart's opera *Don Giovanni,*" he said matter-of-factly, shrugging. Then he chuckled. "So why not have Mozart in my clown musical about Don Juan?"

"It's theft, for one thing."

"It's not theft." Toni threw his fork down, laughing. He pointed at her. "Only you'd say that. Mozart didn't end his opera with a clown atop a pedestal."

He has a point there. "But you used his work to conclude yours. His conclusion. His music. His art."

"All art is theft, Mina. The best is what you steal from life." He picked up the fork and pointed it at her. "Anyway, it was the perfect finale."

"A clown falling to his death, singing *Don Giovanni*?"

"No, a harlequin taking off a clown *mask*, singing a eulogy before death. Remember the end of Act II of *Don Giovanni*? Don Giovanni faces a statue for the sins of his past. Yeah? The play, which is largely a comedy, becomes a masterful statement of life and death. Don Giovanni refuses to repent for all the sexual conquests of his life. He is threatened by the statue and told he will go to hell if he does not repent, but he ignores the warning. That would be against his nature. He is a libertine, no? More so, he is human. And so he falls. In so doing, Mozart takes light opera and turns it into a piece of pure genius. That is art that touches God."

"And what does that have to do with *your* play?"

"It, it, it ..." He stared pensively outside at the view for a moment and then took a deep breath, turning and looking into her eyes.

She had always loved his eyes. They were hazel and almond shaped, under bushy but well-groomed brows.

He smiled. "It's a show of sensuality. A dance with a clown and ballerinas on stage. It's, of course, absurd, as the clowns are dressed in white baggy pants and in clown face. Ridicolo. But that draws you to watch. Why do lovely clowns dance around the Harlequin? And, of course, all dance is sex."

She raised her brow at that.

"By the end of my play, the clown sits atop a pedestal and tempts a fall. That temptation excites everyone. That is life. Death at any moment. It draws them to look and listen to me."

"Which you love," she interjected with a chuckle.

"Which allows the Harlequin to sing. But, it ... it, it is not only the end of *Don Giovanni*; it is a harlequin singing *Don Giovanni*. A clown close to you and me. Not just a libertine, a clown. A mask. Us."

"Do you two know what you'd like this evening?"

Toni jerked in his chair and turned to the waiter standing beside the table. He had been so engrossed in explaining his play that the man had surprised him.

"We have a special dish tonight. Crab-stuffed shrimp with a pepper sauce. Absolutely delicious."

"La bistecca alla fiorentina, please," Toni said in his exquisite Italian accent. "I'd like that. How about you, Mina?" he asked with a wink. "Do you remember our evening in Naples?"

"Oh, Toni," she said, laughing. Then she leaned forward. "How do you remember that?" She turned to the waiter. "I'll have your Florentine steak too. And …" She searched the menu some more and pointed at a side dish. "With this side. The mac and cheese."

"Excellent choice," the waiter said.

For a flash, she caught him wrinkling his nose. It didn't seem like the macaroni and cheese was an excellent choice to him at all.

"The food here is fabulous," Mina said, enjoying her salad.

"Si."

Mina smiled at Toni's dismissal.

He had another taste and put his fork down again. "A human falls, no? Literally, Mina, the clown dies. The symbolism becomes direct metaphor. We live, we love, we die."

"On Broadway?"

"Of course." He nodded. "On Broadway. The threat of the Harlequin's fall clinches it. It's why people will come. They're going to wait for the platform to sway or for a foot to slip. The rest, the depth, nobody cares. I brought the fun of the Big Top under the sway of Mozart. And what better composer to showcase such a feat of brilliance. Those around him said Mozart laughed like a clown." And then, indeed, Toni laughed just like a clown. He struck his chest with his hand and acted with silly bravado, like the performer in her dream. "Ridicolo. Divertente! Mozart e Antonio Vollini!" Then he burst into laughter.

"You're so conceited." Mina laughed while dabbing her mouth with her napkin. "I can't believe you."

He just nodded.

"It's adorable." She touched his hand.

"Food is food. A face is a face. You can do what you will to hide it, Mina, but ultimately you are what you are underneath. God gave us purity. It is what we choose to cover it that leads to our fall."

He grabbed some bread, pushed it into his mouth, and said, "Mina, tell me, I thought you said on the phone that you were dancing at the university? What do you mean you haven't danced in a long time?"

Uh-oh. "I'm modeling. Not dancing."

"I see."

She touched his hand again. "I'd be honored to dance in your play. If you want me to. Crazy or not, it's your play. I warn you, I haven't danced in years. But I've always loved your work."

"With clowns?" he asked, looking down at her hand with a playful grin.

"Yes. Clowns, Toni."

She sighed and forced a look out the window again. It was just a gorgeous view of skyscrapers and twinkling lights. Her heart quickened, but not out of fear this time. She was going to get a job tonight. She knew it! That's why she had gotten all dressed up. She had been excited to see her friend, but the prospect of working on a play on Broadway excited her so much more.

She shook her head and turned back to him. He wasn't eating. He seemed to be watching her.

"A clown singing *Don Giovanni*," she said, shaking her head. "Why not? The Big Top and Mozart? On Broadway."

"We're ar-*tists*," he said. "You sing. You dance. You paint. Hell, you know more about classical music than I do. You know Bach provided foundation, Mozart colored it, and Beethoven hammered it in. Their best works touch God."

"And you think your art touches God, Toni?"

"I know it does. This will be like the mac 'n cheese you ordered with our Florentine steak. In this restaurant. Food is food, Mina. That is my play."

She paused in thought and then nodded. "So you're throwing mac 'n cheese all over Broadway?"

"Esattamente," he said with a chuckle, holding his arms wide open again. "You got it. I knew, of all people, you would."

"No, Toni, I don't." She furrowed her brow and shook her head. "I don't get it. I really don't understand it at all."

"I think you do." He turned stern, leaning back in his seat, and folded his arms again. "And it will be the number-one show on Broadway … *if* you help me."

"How can I help you?"

"I want you to be in my play. Can you? What modeling job are you doing? What agency are you using?"

"I'm a model for art students."

He nodded.

"A nude model, Toni."

He furrowed his brow, put his fork down on the plate, and turned to the window. He looked uncomfortably somber for a moment. She had never mentioned it to him on the phone.

"Why me?" she asked. "You need another ballet dancer in the ensemble?"

"Hmm? No. I don't want you in the ensemble. Mina, I told you many years ago, at the institute, what I thought of you. Your face. The way you smile. You have a glow. It's in your blood. You know your great-ancestor, Christine Daaé, was a famous performer in the Palais Garnier. You're a talented dancer … but dancing is not what I want from my Mina Daaé."

"What do you want then?"

"Your voice. You have the voice of an angel. A voice that touches God."

She nodded thoughtfully again. "I haven't sung in a long time, certainly not Mozart. I'm probably more rusty at singing than dancing, even."

"But you did in school. You know the opera. You were in *Don Giovanni*. I would like you to help with my show. So how 'bout it? Do you want to be in my mac and cheese play on Broadway?"

"I said I did. Of course. What will I be singing?"

"Don Giovanni, of course." He gestured with wide-open arms. "You're to have the starring role as the Harlequin." He smirked. Then after a moment, he laughed more heartily than ever.

She dropped her fork and it clanged on the fine china. A few people from other tables turned. Then she heard herself gasp and felt her face flush and her eyes bulge.

Of course, Toni didn't lose his smile. He laughed harder than ever.

"Is this a joke?"

"No, I'm quite serious. You're a star, Mina. I've always known it. Now that it's my play, I consider myself lucky to be the one debuting you." He reached for her hand, but she pushed it away.

"What's wrong?"

"I thought the Harlequin was a man's role?" she said, staring at the table. "I read it. He has women accusing him of being a libertine. A Don Juan."

"I've changed that. Now they're men accusing you. And women too."

"You're absolutely crazy, you know that?"

"Si." And he took a deep breath. "Mina, I know your voice and I've seen you dance. It's my play and my choice. But

I also know you're the only one crazy enough to refuse. So—I ask you again and, truly, as your good friend, I urge that you say yes to me—this is the chance of a lifetime, and I can't offer it to you again. Will you perform as the Harlequin in my play? You will be my main character. The Harlequin. On Broadway. We open in three months. Do you accept?"

"For sure," she said, throwing her long hair back.

Then it became oddly quiet. Too quiet.

He lost his smile and became strangely contemplative, nodding and turning back to their view—much as he had after she'd told him she was a nude model. She just stared at the flickering candle on the table.

She had been nervous about what he'd intended for the meeting, but she never would have guessed this. The starring role? She really thought that because he was moving to the States he just wanted to see her again—perhaps become closer to her. And maybe he'd offer her a bit part that would make her some money. And she would have been happy with that. But this, this was different. The starring role?

She risked a gaze out the window again with him. It was still just the lovely Manhattan skyline. But when she saw how high up they were, she didn't want to look there either.

"Isn't it an insult for a woman to play a clown?"

"Che?" he asked, furrowing his brow. "No, no, no. Do not think that. I told you that the head clown can be either male or female. The clown covers who she truly is. Not a fool. A mask. With you, a woman. But you of all people—Mina, if you perform it, I will never disrespect you. Not you, my jewel. Of course, you are to be a female Don Juan. A female lost in lust. You are fallible and you shall fall, just as my man did in Paris. But as for you being a clown, I would never dare cover your face. I shall be discreet. For why would I foolishly cover such beauty?"

"Oh, stop." She laughed.

"Mina, you will be dressed like a Pierrot, but I will barely cover you. I will not disrespect you. Everyone in my play is a

clown." He pointed to people at the other tables. "Because …
after all, every single one of us is."

"But I don't care for heights."

"But you will soar, my dear."

After sipping some red wine, she said, "Mind telling me
why *me?*"

"I already have. Your voice touches God. We shall receive
ovations from heaven!" He drank some wine, laughing, but
then became stern. He lifted a finger, just like he had atop the
pedestal in her dream, reached back into his blazer on the
seat, and took out a single red rose. He handed the flower to
her. "Mina, my jewel, you shall steal the sound and sight of
angels and bring them down to Broadway for every clown to
see and hear."

MANNEQUIN

MINA DIDN'T LIKE HER JOB. SHE WASN'T ASHAMED OF NUDE modeling per se; she was more ashamed that her ambitions in dance and theater ended in modeling. That's why she had felt ashamed when she told her former instructor, Toni, about it. It seemed like her life was a dead end — until last night at dinner with him.

Nude modeling was the most lucrative job she could find. It paid well, and soon the students, even the new ones, didn't seem to pay any more attention to her than they would a mannequin. Her boss—a very nice, short, Asian woman with small, thick glasses named Ms. Kuni—was one of the sweetest ladies she had ever known. Ms. Kuni was sensitive, unlike her instructor a year before. On her first job, the teacher embarrassed the hell out of her by walking up close, touching her boobs with a stick, and gliding it along her ribs down to her ass. Ms. Kuni never disrespected her.

The worst part of her job now was not embarrassment; it was physical demand. She had to remain in the same position, like a statue, for fifteen, even thirty minutes at a time.

Today, on a very hot summer morning as the students settled down with their paints, Mina stood beside her stool, holding her long black hair back behind her head and looking straight out in no particular direction. Ms. Kuni liked this position because it accentuated Mina's firm breasts. She could feel the students' eyes tracing her hips, the curvature of her breasts and tanned and flat nipples, and her arms. Since it was such a scorcher outside, her sweat likely helped accentuate the lines of her body. Then there was the pyramid formed between her two breasts at mid-chest. It was so quiet that she could hear the brushstrokes. She imagined them touching the shadows of her belly and her ribs. Then drawing the small hole of her belly button. Next they'd fill it in, softening the lines a bit to mimic her smooth skin.

She saw her reflection in a large mirror from the corner of her eye. Her forehead was a little larger than the norm. Her nose was a bit sharper. Her lower red lip was a little thicker than the upper one. The students would be painting her face, too.

It was not such a terrible job. She could focus inward on her problems or just think of nothing at all as she posed. Perhaps meditate, as she had learned to do, and focus on her breathing. And the benefit was she could do all this while getting paid.

Cocking her head back ever so slightly, to look away, she saw students touching up her body and shading it with brushes.

Ms. Kuni signaled for Mina to change positions.

Mina sat down on the stool and leaned forward while covering her breasts with her arms. She liked this position, because now she could look into their eyes. They were shy, too. All of them avoided her gaze while painting.

In the front row was a tanned boy dressed in a T-shirt and shorts. She imagined he was from California or Florida. A surfer. She studied his body, for—it was a secret—later at home, she used the students for her artwork just as they used her.

His nose was like hers, sharp but short, and she could see

it wrinkle in the middle as he worked, brushing her on the canvas. He had a strong forehead, a faint dimple on his chin, thin, light-red lips, and chiseled cheekbones. He wore a white cotton tank top, but she could see the lines along his muscular chest and upper arms. She could imagine the skin along the ripples of his abdomen. She pictured what it would be like tracing and painting an image of his skin over the angles of his deltoids and biceps with her own brush. Then she looked down at his jeans. He sat uncomfortably on his own stool, frequently rising to dab paint in different directions, while gazing at her. Having him stand, she would run the lines down around his well-developed quads and the tight crack of his ass. The athletic hardness would be easy enough to recreate. The subtlety of the softness of his stomach and ass would be the real challenge.

"Fifteen more minutes," said Ms. Kuni. Then she crouched down and looked at Mina with a sweet smile. "Are you doing okay, Mina? Can you do fifteen more?"

"Sure."

At the end of class, Mina threw on her white robe, which had been lying on a chair by the curtain, and ran to the door before her teacher left.

"Ms. Kuni," Mina said. "Ms. Kuni." Everyone else was gathering their things to leave too.

"Yes?"

"This is my last class."

"Oh. All right." She adjusted her glasses and looked up at Mina with a sweet smile. "Thank you for coming, dear." She didn't seem too surprised. Mina knew people had come in and out of this job many times before. "Did you tell Dr. Ruthers?"

Mina nodded.

"Did you find a modeling job elsewhere?"

"No. I'm spending my time in a play. You never know. It could be a big break. Or I could be back. We'll see how it goes."

"A play." Ms. Kuni smiled kindly. "Oh, yes, you said when you started that you liked theater."

"Really? I don't remember."

"I do. When I showed you our classroom. I hope your successor is as disciplined as you. You know, the girl before you was always late and she was always taking too many breaks." Her teacher shook her head, and Mina laughed. "You've been perfect."

"Thanks, Ms. Kuni."

"Hey, you're not going anywhere." Her friend Gail sprinted into the room, pushing her way past two students making for the door. She was a pretty girl with long blonde hair and a pale complexion. "You best not be." Gail was fun, and Mina liked her. Always smiley, like her friend Toni, Gail was the type of person to never be angry over anything. Except now.

"Hi, Gail. I didn't see you."

"Oh, I was…" She opened her large eyes wide and looked nervously at Ms. Kuni, who readjusted her spectacles and cocked her head back in irritation. "In the back. You didn't see me? I was tracing you, Mina." When Ms. Kuni turned back to Mina, Gail waved her hands back and forth to get Mina's attention. "Where are you going, anyway?" she asked.

"She said a play, Gail." Ms. Kuni looked at Gail over her glasses. "And where were you this morning?"

"In the back row," Gail lied, nodding.

"Show me your work tomorrow. I think you just came in. I don't think you were here during class at all."

"She was," Mina lied. "I saw her when I was standing."

"You were standing at the beginning of class," Ms. Kuni replied, raising her eyebrows. "She was definitely not here when we started."

Gail put her hands on her hips and opened her eyes wide, behind her teacher, pissed at Mina.

Mina chuckled. She couldn't help it.

"Your finished work tomorrow, Gail," said the teacher.

"And I already collected the work from yesterday, so if you come up short, I'll know." Then she put a hand on Mina's arm and said with a sweet grin, "Bye, Mina. Thanks so much for helping me teach our painters."

When the door shut and the teacher left, Gail and Mina were alone.

Gail whirled around. "Fuck, can't you lie a little bit better?"

"Sorry."

"Well, I've been sketching your figure for weeks. I'm sure I'll remember your tits and ass. I can probably sketch you in my sleep tonight."

"All right, Gail," Mina replied with a chuckle.

Gail smiled. "Where are you going? What's this about leaving? What sort of play?"

"It's *The Harlequin*. It opens on Broadway in a few months."

Gail's mouth opened and her large eyes grew wider. She froze. She was speechless. And that wasn't like her at all.

Mina felt like closing Gail's eyes and mouth. "You okay, Gail?"

"Bullshit."

"It's true."

"Bullshit."

"I'm not joking."

"I thought you said you weren't dancing anymore?"

"A good friend came to town from Paris. He's the producer. He offered me a role. The starring role."

"Shut the fuck up."

"Gail, stop swearing." Mina walked behind the curtain. "I'm gonna get dressed."

"Let's go to lunch so you can tell me all about it."

"All right."

There was silence and, as Mina got dressed, she reflected that this could very well be the last time she dressed in the art room. She hoped it would be. She was sweating terribly from the heat, and she didn't like putting her clothes on over her wet body. She buttoned her blouse, thinking her young friend could have left—Gail had become so quiet—but then she heard a voice say, "It's hot as hell, isn't it, Mina?"

"Yes."

"Do you remember that boy who liked you? Rhett. The tall guy with the tattoos of lizards all over his neck. You know, the one we saw at the bar last week. Remember? He's the one who had the ponytail. He liked you. He kept talking to you as you sucked on your beer. Do you remember him, Mina?"

"Yeah. What about him?"

"He's going to a party tomorrow and he invited me. And you know what he said?"

"No. What?"

She laughed. "He said to ask my radiant friend to come. *Radiant.* Funny, huh? Can you believe that?"

"What's so funny about that?"

"He wasn't the kinda guy to say that kind of word. I was surprised he even knew what the fuck *radiant* meant. He was a bit of a moron. Cute, though. But he couldn't recall your name. I thought it was fun because he asked for you to come with me. My *radiant* friend."

"Oh. Okay. Maybe."

"What do you mean, maybe?" She actually sounded hurt.

"I'm sorry, Gail, but Toni hasn't told me yet when rehearsals begin. If I'm needed Friday, I can't come."

There was a mirror beside the curtain, and she took out a comb from her handbag and ran it through her hair while gazing at her reflection. Then she cleaned some smudges of runny mascara and sweat from under her eyes.

"Toni, huh? And … what's this Toni like? Is he cute?"

"Gail, why do you think all men are just here for a date?"

"Because I'm not old like you."

"Well," she said with a laugh. "I suppose he's cute. But he's fifty."

"Oh."

"Uh-huh." Mina walked around the curtain and smiled at her friend.

"You're not really leaving, are you?" Gail asked.

Mina lost her smile looking at Gail's expression. "Stop. Broadway's in Manhattan, not LA. We can still hang out."

"For sure," Gail said with a nod and a tight grin. Gail looked depressed as hell.

So Mina extended her arms out wide and gave her friend a big hug.

THE PEDESTAL

"WHAT WOULD YOU LIKE ME TO SING?"

Mina heard her voice echo through the empty hall. A few curious people backstage turned at her question. As the lights shone on her, she squinted. She couldn't see Toni or the rest of them, but she knew they were in the center of the third row, staring at her just as they had stared at the redheaded singer who had auditioned that morning.

"*Zaide.*" Toni's Italian accent was amplified by his microphone. "Sing *Zaide*. You know, our favorite: 'Tender Is My Smile.' You know the one. We performed that one countless times."

"I know the song, Toni," she replied with a nod. It was "Ruhe Sanft," which meant "rest in peace." A lovely song from Mozart's unfinished opera *Zaide*. But she didn't want to sing it after hearing the exquisite voice of the redhead singing it earlier.

How can I sing better than that?

"The orchestra will play. You sing. You remember the German, no?"

"Yes."

And she waited for the orchestra to begin.

The amphitheater looked like it was capable of seating over a thousand. Old-fashioned and opulent, with a giant polished wood stage and old seats covered in velvet, matching the red satin curtains on the stage, it held a power all its own. It was as if the architect had made a building so grand it moved the crowds even without a performance. The balconies and great crystal chandeliers above her appeared to have been there for a hundred years. She loved the yellow webbed design on the red carpet, the decorative wooden columns, and even the modern neon-purple lighting along the ceiling rafters. But the strangest thing, the thing that really disturbed Mina, was that she recognized it all. Certainly, the theater was old. Perhaps she had seen pictures on the internet? But it was more than that. This fit her dream… No, it perfectly mirrored it.

Beside the stage, a few stagehands ran about while three girls in bright-red pancake tutus marked their dance steps. One dancer dipped down, touching her toes, another was putting on pointe shoes, and the third was moving her hands and feet in ballet positions.

The flute and violins began playing a lovely composition from *Zaide*.

Mina looked down and tightly clutched the microphone. She hadn't sung in so long, but as she heard her cue from the music, she performed and that finally relaxed her.

Her voice rang out, surprisingly strong. It bounced off the walls—the acoustics in the building were perfect. Throughout the hall, all she could hear was her voice, and it was lovely in the magnificent theater. She sang to them as if she had planned the performance for months but, of course, she'd had no preparation at all. She probably hadn't sung on stage since she was in Paris. Certainly, her performance was not as good as, if not far inferior to, the woman she had seen when she first arrived. But they didn't tell her to stop.

Mina looked around the auditorium as she sang; dancers were warming up backstage. They were no longer stretching.

They were gazing at her, frozen, as if in surprise. Had she done something stupid?

As the song ended, she looked down at the producers, shielding her eyes from the glare of the lights. There was no clapping. No applause.

Then she heard the sound of a microphone being tapped. "Bring the platforms." It was Toni's Italian accent. There was some objection from below, and he snapped something inaudible in Italian. "Bring the pedestals. Mina, I want you to lead the song in our last act, the final act in *Don Giovanni*, up on the platform. Can you do that? I want to show them this. You see, they're still a bit twitchy about my show."

"But a male voice leads the song."

"No matter. I'd like you to sing it. We spoke of this."

"But … it's a baritone accompaniment, Toni. It's famous as—"

"Yeah, yeah. I can't wait to hear *you* do it."

Mina waited for them to arrange the stage. She must have sung well, otherwise they probably would have hauled her off. Or perhaps she'd sounded so awful that Toni was trying desperately to save her by having her sing another song? She didn't know. But the dancers and stagehands stopped what they were doing and sat in chairs, curled up on the floor, or leaned against the wall to watch her. Everyone did. They all waited as a giant tower was rolled onto the center of the stage. And a group of people in black clothes were tying a net to the two platforms. Then another tower was rolled onto the other side of the stage. The towers were tightrope platforms, though no tightrope was being hung.

"Mina, I told you this was a rehearsal, no?" Toni asked. His amplified voice echoed through the hall.

"Yes."

"Well, I need you to sing the last act for my friends. Some of them will not be here tomorrow. Can you do that for them?" He sounded so serious.

"Did … did you like the way I sang *Zaide*?"

Toni chuckled. "This is not an audition, Mina. Please climb the steps above us and sing. If you look down, you'll see the entire orchestra accompanying you."

"I just sing—"

"Yeah, yeah."

"All right."

Mina climbed the ladder and looked up. The platform seemed to touch the dark-purple lit ceiling. But Mina had read the screenplay. She knew the Harlequin had to deal with heights. She wondered if this was another reason she was so shaky this morning.

As she climbed the last few steps on the ladder, her feet trembled. Then she was stupid enough to look down. She was no longer blinded by the light, but Toni and the other producers seemed so far below. She could see the orchestra pit too. It was full. So many people had gathered to perform this morning. For her?

She got to the top and it was worse. It was a narrow platform with a microphone tied to a metal pole. Mina found it hard to swallow. Her heart raced. Somehow, she managed to climb the last step and kneel on the ledge. She didn't dare look down at the stage below.

"Are you at the top?" Toni asked.

"Yes." She was surprised to hear her voice shake.

"Turn the spotlight on her," Toni directed.

It was bright again and Mina shifted in surprise, feeling a rise by her butt and her familiar terror of falling. Her legs shook violently. She crouched down and carefully moved her legs, one at a time, over the ledge. She wondered if her heart would explode from all the stress. What an odd combination of excitement and fear. But … if she could just finish this … this "rehearsal"—which she now knew full well was a complete farce—if she could do that, she might win a lead position on Broadway. On Broadway, her life dream.

The orchestra rang out with the familiar drums and violins. The rumble made Mina more nervous, as the vibration shook the steel platform. Then she prepared to sing "Don Giovanni."

She knew the song. Just like *Zaide*, she had sung it in the university in Paris. But that was school and so many years ago. And that was accompanying a male Don Juan, never leading the aria.

When it came time for her to sing, she fell mum. The orchestra stopped.

"What's the matter?" Toni asked through his microphone.

"Uh … you want me to start the song with the music—"

"The lead role, Mina. I do."

"The baritone section? The part of the accuser?"

"Si."

"In … low notes?"

"No, no," Toni said with a laugh. "In your same lovely tenor."

Mina swallowed. "But … it doesn't feel right. It's not supposed to be like that."

"Portami pazienza. What do you mean, it doesn't feel right?"

She didn't know Italian, but she guessed what he meant.

"Mina," Toni said, clearing his throat, "this is not the best time to discuss this."

That was an understatement.

"Well, I mean, it's not just the change in voice. You're asking me to sing the accusation. But I thought the Harlequin was acting as Don Juan. Why am I the accuser?"

"Try it. *You* lead the song. *You* accuse. There are other singers you can't see who will provide additional vocals to defend. Everything is reversed again. It will work. Most in the audience will not know what you know. This is for effect. Trust me."

"But, shouldn't—"

"Mina, the musicians are waiting. They've all come to hear your wonderful voice this morning. Can you do this?"

That question was terrible, because if she said no, she would probably lose the part.

"Play the music," Mina said.

"You make me so very happy," Toni said.

It didn't sound like she did. And that was the first time ever that Mina wasn't fond of his expression.

The music in D minor thundered. Once again, it was so powerful that it shook the foundation of her narrow platform. Her legs shook over the hundred-foot precipice, and her body trembled.

When it was time, Mina sang. She sang "Don Giovanni." And, once more, she liked the sound of her voice with the orchestration, even though the piece sounded very different with her high notes. Then she was shocked to hear a male voice accompanying her. As she sang, she looked down. Toni's seat was empty. He was walking to center stage, holding a microphone and singing. In Mozart's play, his voice would have represented Don Giovanni and his companion defending himself from her, the accuser. But in this rendition, as he stood on stage pointing up at her, Toni's hand gestures were at times contrary to his actual words. He was pointing at her as if she were Don Juan while defending himself, as if he were Don Juan, with his vocals. The whole thing was backward and confused. The actions were reversed. On purpose? But would anyone watching the play who didn't know the words in Italian even notice? Or indeed, as Toni had said, even care?

Mina let go of all concerns and allowed herself to get lost in song. Even the accusations became robotic. It was as if she had left her body. And she loved it. She enjoyed accusing him. It felt powerful. She wondered if this was why Toni had set it up this way. It was so powerful that she almost stood up with excitement, forgetting her fear of heights. It was as if her voice and Toni's fought one another, but really they comple-mented each other. Neither missed a note. Neither missed a tone. It was exquisite. She wasn't sure how she sounded to her critics, but she enjoyed the thunder of the orchestra and the sound of Toni's voice. She didn't even mind the vibrations in the steel platform anymore.

As it was coming to a close, a spotlight fell on the other pedestal, across the stage. A singer in Pierrot clown face, but wearing a black cape and a black mask, appeared on the other side. He reminded her of Toni in clown face in her dream. And now this clown pantomimed silently to the sound of both of their voices, swaying his arms in time with the music. The clown reached out a hand to her. Was this another one of Toni's surprises? Toni just kept singing.

Then Mina recognized this clown. She recognized the shiny black ceramic mask covering half of his face. It was the mask of the handsome man in her dream. And then she remembered his soft gloves. But, instead of facing the empty auditorium, he looked at her, miming her words in silence. He gestured with wide arms for her to rise. And she obeyed, while singing to him and Toni. All three clowns sang now. Then, as the final notes of the piece played, she stood up straight, no longer fearing the height. She reached out to touch his hand.

And here is where I fall.

REST IN PEACE

Bright lights danced, some red, blue, and purple, swirling around her and waking her from tranquil peace. There were flashes of yellow light as she focused on faces hovering over her. She blinked her eyes. She touched her aching forehead. Then she looked behind the faces and saw the steel platform, now towering over her. She was on her back. All the lights were on. And a bunch of performers whose acquaintance she had just made, and many she had seen backstage, were huddled over her.

"My God, Mina, are you okay?" Toni knelt over her, holding her hand.

"What happened?" she asked. Someone helped her sit up. Another ran over with a cup of water. She took it, but her hand shook terribly. She handed it back to Toni without drinking it. "What happened?"

"You fell. Into the net, thank God. Why did you do that? Are you all right?"

"I'm fine." Mina lay back down. "I … don't like heights. I just fell. That's all. I'm okay."

She thought about the man on the other side of the theater. She turned and searched for him. Where was he? He had fallen, too. The man in her dreams. The man with the mask.

"Should we call 911?" a dancer asked.

Someone helped her sit up and leaned her against a large pillow. Then Toni pushed the cup of water back into her hand. She sipped it.

"I'm okay," Mina said to everyone hovering over her. "Really, I am. But … how did I do, Toni? Did you like the way I sang?"

"Young lady…" A gray-haired woman with a crew cut crouched beside her with a smile. Mina had been introduced to her earlier; Daniella was their lead choreographer. "If you sing like that live, during the show, our production will be a smash," the choreographer said.

"Yeah, Dani." Toni nodded. "Yeah. Incredible, Mina. I told you."

"Well, I'm more interested in balletomanes," Daniella added. "I can work her feet. But that was stupid. Real dumb, Toni. You shouldn't have had her up there so soon."

Toni nodded.

"Your voice is amazing, Mina," said a white-haired, dark-skinned man above her. He had been introduced earlier as Vince, the main coproducer. "I really hope you'll join our production."

Mina sipped more water. All the anxiety of the morning left her and she felt fine. No, she felt better than fine. She felt happy. They liked her singing. They were asking her to join them based on her "rehearsal." She felt wonderful.

"But Toni, is the other performer all right?"

Toni furrowed his brow.

MORTE

MINA WAS OUTSIDE HER OWN BODY, WATCHING, AS A DIM GRAY light cast a shadow over pale skin. Her black lips cracked open ever so slightly. They opened and closed rhythmically—as undulating breaths emerged in a mist—as if in song, as she lay on top of wrinkled white sheets. But she couldn't move. Behind her bed, through her wall, were shadows of trees and a dirt trail that meandered among thick brush and bushes beside a small stream. She could hear the trickling water. And a full moon lit the shadowed forest behind the wall.

There was music. Wolfgang Amadeus Mozart: the start of Mozart's "Requiem."

Fingers slowly crept along her belly, tracing her belly button, gliding along her naked skin, and making its way under the curves of her breasts, pressing deeper, and then touching her leaden-colored nipples. Her nipples were hard and she felt aroused, but she couldn't see the fingers touching her. It was too dark. She could barely see herself.

"You were the singer on the pedestal?" she asked. "The man I saw fall with me?"

"Oui."

She heard that recognizable French accent again.

Then he appeared, clearly visible, standing over the bed—the man with the mask. But that was all he wore. He was nude, and behind him and what once was the wall in her bedroom was the woods, still shrouded in darkness. The mask covered half of his face, revealing part of a thin goatee. His face, what she could see, was handsome. His fingers slid delicately, like flowing water in a forest stream, down her side, over her soft skin.

The view changed. Still outside her body, with everything gray and black, she watched herself under him on the bed. His broad, muscular shoulders and his powerful arms and legs flexed over her. His ass rose and fell as he thrust into her, straddling her body. As he moved, one powerful hand grasped the bedsheets as the other pulled her closer to him. She felt the pleasure between her legs, though she still watched from the ceiling. She felt every hard thrust from his tight, muscular physique and the wetness and tingles of pleasure inside.

The view changed again. His lips pressed against her passionately now, and she felt the stubbles of his beard as he ran it along her lips while gliding his hand down her naked hip. She moaned from another hard thrust. He fucked her, over and over, while firmly sucking her bottom lip. His other hand wandered under her side and along the crack of her ass.

"What's your name?" she asked breathlessly between kisses. "Tell me. Please, tell me your name."

"Je suis la mort transcendante."

"Tell me. Please tell me … Please."

"Erik."

She was under him now, his eyes so close to hers. She remembered those emeralds sparkling in the light, and even illuminated by rays of moonlight, they glowed jade. She ran her hand along the open side of his mask and then up along the thin hair of his head. She pressed up into him, and he gave a satisfied groan. He was handsome, so handsome, but he wore that black mask. Why? Why should he cover such a gorgeous face? She wanted it off. She wanted him completely, his face and body, with nothing covering him.

She grabbed him and turned him on his side. As he pressed deep inside her, she grabbed his mask, trying to take it off. He turned his face away but brought her close to him again. She tried to pull off the mask once more.

"No," he snapped, snatching her wrist. "No, Christine."

"But why?"

"Je suis Don Juan."

He thrust inside her hard, as if punishing her, then squeezed her wrist and twisted it.

"Oww. Erik, stop it. You're hurting me."

"Ne retirez pas le masque tant que vous n'êtes pas prêt."

"I am ready. Please, Erik. I want to see you."

Darkness.

A light shone on five dancers in clown face, moving slowly, with hands held over their heads. The dreary gray faded and light became vibrant. Colorful. Bright. A rainbow shone over the five dancers as they danced. Mina recognized this as the stage of the Harlequin. Three women wearing long, fluffy blue and saffron dresses, with tall, white headdresses, danced with two men in gray coats, breeches, and white wigs. They swayed back and forth, smiling behind painted frowns, on the wooden stage as an orchestra played. The music was still the "Requiem" by Mozart.

Her head turned from the stage and she saw Erik. Just like in her dream, he was watching the play with her, but this time, they lay on their sides together, naked. She admired his rippled abs and muscular arms, and his bright-green eyes gazed into hers while he ran his fingers over her breasts and fucked her. He cradled her tightly, as if not wanting her to get away. The seats in the auditorium were gone. Only a single bed lay in front of the stage. And as he pressed into her, still fucking her, they watched the play.

Mina felt embarrassed. But she didn't get up. They were in public, but in an empty auditorium. Something about the weirdness of that made her not disengage. Or was it the pleasure?

As they fucked, the dancers paid no attention, continuing their trot back and forth, back and forth, with hands held high, strutting to orchestral music.

"Stop. Stop it now, Erik. I'm scared. It's … it's indecent."

She looked away from the stage and stared at those bright-green eyes. Then he breathed heavily beside her ear but didn't say anything.

His tongue ran along her neck and he grasped her more tightly. She tried to look away, but she couldn't turn from him. She couldn't look anywhere. So she buried her head in a soft pillow. Part of her wanted to get away, but the other part didn't.

She was afraid. She was scared that she wouldn't be good enough. That she couldn't sing. That she couldn't dance. Surely, she couldn't perform as well as these dancers on stage. She wasn't good enough for Broadway. She knew that. And she was afraid that they would find out and see that she was a failure.

"Stop," she said. "Stop, Erik. Stop it now. That's enough."

"No."

She looked up as the actors, in clown face and colonial dress, continued to trot forward and back, forward and back, amidst the music of Mozart.

"Who are you?" she demanded, turning from him and closing her eyes. "You must tell me. Tell me now, Erik. Stop and tell me." And when he didn't, she felt trapped and cried out, "Stop! *Stop it!*"

He finally let go and she pushed herself off.

"Why the mask?" She touched the half-mask. It felt metallic and cold. "Why?" It was pitch black, so dark that it felt like emptiness itself. She felt like if she reached in, her hand would fall inside. "Please. You're frightening me. Tell me."

She tugged at the mask but he snatched her wrist again and twisted it hard.

"Je suis le Don Juan triomphant! Je suis mort! Morte, Christine Daaé!"

Mina jerked. Her eyes opened in pitch darkness. Her hands clutched wrinkled sheets. Only a dim light appeared, from a crack in the window by the wall. The darkness made her more uneasy. And it was quiet, with only the humming of her refrigerator. She breathed heavily and felt wet from perspiration.

She looked around until her eyes fell upon a painting of a screaming face on an easel beside her mattress. And next to that was an image of a naked man with arms being stretched, gashes with dripping blood, and a face with gnashing teeth and eyes squeezed tight while being tortured on a rack. She took a deep breath. These were her works of art, but her subject matter wasn't making her feel any better.

When she sat up, she was surprised to see that she was naked. That was weird. Usually she wore a camisole and panties to bed. Or when cold, a nightgown. Never naked. She took another deep breath; then she forced herself up and turned on the light.

All the easels and canvases leaning on the walls disturbed her. Seeing her art—demons, vampires, mutilation, and torture—beside her bed after her dream was the last thing she needed. Then she furrowed her brow. On a pillow was a single red rose. She picked it up and clutched it to her chest. It was so important to her. It was as if it was some magical charm against all the darkness. But how did it get there?

She remembered. It was the rose Toni had gifted her at the restaurant in honor of her accepting the role in his musical.

THE ACCIDENT

THE FIRST DAY MINA DID NOT SHOW UP FOR REHEARSAL, SHE told herself she wasn't feeling well. She spent the whole day in her apartment, sitting on a couch, eating chips, drinking Coke, and staring at her TV. Sometimes the screen was on, sometimes it wasn't. It didn't matter. She didn't want to do anything. She told herself she needed a respite after falling a hundred feet. And why wouldn't she? The very last thing she wanted to do was climb that ladder again.

The second day she used the same excuse.

But on the third day, she started looking at her rather paltry pantry. And she thought of Ms. Kuni.

It was on the third day, in the afternoon—while binging on reruns of her favorite classic TV shows, *Gilligan's Island* and *Bewitched*—that she heard a knock on her door. She jumped from her couch and looked down at her red silk robe. It would have to do. She touched her hair. Of course, her long, dark hair looked like a bird's nest and she had no makeup on. She hoped it was her friend Gail. It probably was.

She looked through the peephole in her entryway and saw that it was her second guess. A man with a beard in a brown beanie, white button-down, and dark slacks was standing outside her door.

"Hi, Toni."

"Mina." He flashed a fake smile. Then he peered behind her and removed his hat, scratching his head. "Mind if I come in?"

"How'd you find me?"

"Mina, I've been sending you Christmas and birthday cards for years." Then, for a flash, he looked like the old Toni, with a jovial grin, as he put his beanie back over his head and walked through the door. She shyly ran her hand over the knots in her hair. He didn't seem to notice. He seemed too busy looking over her apartment disapprovingly.

Actually, she was quite proud of her place. It was a nice pad for Manhattan. The kitchen and living room formed a single-studio unit, and there was a small room, if you'd call it one, off to the side—her bedroom and art studio. It was close to the university, and it was cheap and rather spacious for New York.

Toni sat down on her ratty beige couch. Then he smiled at the TV. Jeannie was on the screen, in her silly pink genie getup, in the classic sitcom *I Dream of Jeannie*.

"I see you still have the same taste in shows."

"Only the best. You want some coffee?"

"No, I'm okay."

No time for coffee? Hmm. Boy, he must really be mad.

She felt him watch her as she walked over to the other side of the couch, yawning and stretching, and sat down. She leaned forward, folding her arms over her lap, and faced him.

He put a finger to his chin and said in his thick Italian accent, "You don't look good."

Mina laughed. It was the first time he had ever insulted her appearance. "Sorry, Toni."

"No, I'm sorry. I'm very sorry. I understand. What happened was absolutely terrible. You have every reason to be avoiding us and to be angry with me."

"It wasn't your fault." She shrugged. "I knew the dangers."

He took a deep breath. Then he said very carefully, "If you come back—and I think you know that's why I'm here—I want you to know that you'll be safe. The height is meant to alarm the audience, not you. Once, I'll admit, it wasn't safe, but that was a long time ago in Paris."

He's lying, Christine.

Mina searched the room for a voice that seemed as clear as Toni's. It was a voice with a French accent. The voice of the man who had come to her bed last night.

"Something the matter?" Toni asked.

"No, nothing. Perhaps some music?" Mina asked with a forced smile, grabbing the TV remote off the coffee table.

Toni shrugged. "Whatever you like."

Mina turned the TV channel to a classical radio station. Ironically, it was—

"Herr Mozart," Toni said with a nod. "Coincidence, eh? I wonder?"

"He's a popular composer, Toni."

"Si, but I don't believe in coincidences. No, not like this one." Toni chuckled and nodded, and his laugh made Mina chuckle too. But then Mina wrinkled her nose, recognizing the musical piece. "'Sonata Semplice.' I loathe 'Sonata Semplice.' It has to be the most popular piece of shit Mozart ever wrote."

"Popular like *I Dream of Jeannie?*"

"You have a point there."

"Yes, but only you, my dear, would know the name of Mozart's piece." He took a deep breath, scooted forward on the couch, and looked very stern. "Mina, I'm sorry. So sorry. But I need you to return and attend my rehearsals. You see, I wrote the play for you."

"What do you mean?"

"I wrote *The Harlequin* for you." He took her hand and she felt herself blush. Then he moved closer and pressed her hand between his fingers. She wondered how he could even touch her with her hair looking so ugly. "I mean, not the original performance but the Broadway play. This rendition of *The Harlequin* was made for my star, Mina Daaé. In Paris. I invited you then, but you were set on leaving. But when you told me that you had moved to Manhattan, I suspected your dreams. Was I wrong? Was it not your dream to be in a show on Broadway?"

Mina nodded.

"I made the play for you, Mina. That's the truth. Your grand entrance. My star. I wrote it all for you."

"Because I'm a clown?" She forced a laugh.

"No, because you're a star. You are the so-simple, rare, beautiful bird, so majestic and soaring. Human, yes. A clown. Sure. Like all of us. You will fall. *Figuratively*, my dear. But you are my star. Your voice touches God, Mina. You're an angel."

"Come on, Toni. You've said all this already," Mina said, laughing, and pulled her hand back. "Many times."

"I know, but…" He gently touched her hand again. "I'm serious. Very serious. Vince said he had never heard anything like you before. After hearing you sing, he said that he knows the show will be a hit—if you're in it. Daniella said that, movement or not, your voice is enough for—"

"I'm not sure I like her."

"She's rough around the edges. True. She's gay, you know."

"So?"

"She's a lesbian, Mina. She said that not only is your voice exquisite, so is your body and face. She's attracted to you. I tell you this because … well, we all are. Even if she weren't gay, I think she would find you beautiful. As lovely as your voice. That is why you are my harlequin. That is why I am not. You are a star, Mina. She thought so. She said that she can frame your movements so that we accentuate the motion of your figure in dance. She thinks it can work. But it will take time. And practice. Rehearsal. And—"

"I haven't been dancing. I don't know."

She was surprised at how red his face had become after calling her beautiful. That was so cute. She met his gaze and smiled.

He smiled back, a genuine Toni smile.

"Will you come? Please, Mina. Please. Mina, I can't picture anyone else taking this role. I heard that you saw one of your standbys when you came early. I have a list of singers who can try out for your role. But I say *try*. I don't want them. I want you. Vince and Dani want you, too. It was a rehearsal. I told you this. For you."

"You sang with me. Are you also planning on being in the play?"

"You shall see if you return," he said with a sly grin. "But really, Mina, I'm getting old."

"Not so old." She grasped his hand in both hers and massaged it. Then she leaned against him.

And for a moment they fell silent, staring at the TV screen, sitting quietly beside each other. There was nothing on the TV, just a blue background with music playing. But they sat close, shoulder to shoulder, and just stared at the TV while listening to Mozart. She really liked that.

"Will you come?" he finally repeated, looking again into her eyes. "Please?"

"You're begging," she said with a laugh. "Just stop."

"Si."

"I can try. But, Toni, I'm … scared. I'm afraid of falling. I hate heights. You know that."

What if there's no net? What if it's like it was for me, Christine?

She looked around the room again. She knew the voice was in her head, but it seemed as clear as Toni's.

Toni jumped up and that broke her thoughts. He headed for the door. "Tomorrow morning by seven, okay?" he said. "I'll come by and drive you. You'll meet in the dance room with Daniella while others will practice the first act. She really wants to work on your steps for Act II. Okay?"

"What about the pedestal?"

"With a net, my dear."

He placed a hand on the doorknob. Then he turned and looked at her pensively for a moment.

Mina jumped up and came over. She took his hand and ran the fingers of her other hand along his cheek and over the hairs of his beard. She smiled, looking deeply into his eyes, and gave him a peck on the cheek with her lips. "I'll come. Thank you, Toni. Thanks so much. I mean it."

He nodded sweetly. But then he looked sad.

"What's the matter?" she asked, searching his eyes. "I said I'll go with you, okay? I'll come."

"That's not it."

"What's wrong then?"

He rubbed her fingers and shrugged. "I was afraid you wouldn't open the door."

His hand trembled in hers with those words. He seemed almost coy, which was ridiculous for such a boisterous, extroverted man. Their eyes met, and she felt mesmerized. Like she had with Erik in her dream, but Toni was not a phantom. This was Toni. He was here and now, in the flesh.

"Oh, Toni. Thank you. Thank you for everything." Mina leaned her head against his shoulder. She embraced him and kissed the back of his hand. "You're so sweet."

He remained frozen by the door. She kissed his hand again, and then a couple of fingers. She chuckled and looked up. He was peering at her nervously. She reached up and pecked him on the lips. It was meant as just another goodbye kiss but, somehow, their lips found each other's again. It became more. They stood kissing for a long time by the door. Then she said, almost in a whisper, "Thank you for believing in me."

"You are a star."

She embraced him again and pressed her lips harder against his, her tongue entering his mouth. She desired this. She had never thought of desire with Toni. She knew he had always been attracted to her, but he was her friend. Yet now, she wanted him. Why? Was it because of his play? Or was it those last words: *I was afraid you wouldn't open the door.*

He was unhappy. Why? This was Antonio Vollini, ring-master of the circus, the most happy-go-lucky guy in the world. Now he was sad. Why? Because he had been afraid she wouldn't open the door? Afraid she wouldn't be in his play? Or … was it because he was afraid he would never see her again?

"Tomorrow, okay, Mina?" he said, tearing himself from her embrace.

He turned back and touched the doorknob again, but Mina snatched his arm and turned him toward her. Then she pushed him against the wall. He gasped in surprise. She pressed her lips against his, very hard this time. He jerked back, she figured more from shock than displeasure. She made out with him again.

"Mina," he said between kisses.

"Yes?" She kissed him some more.

"We shouldn't. We're friends."

"I know."

"I don't want anything to happen to that."

"It was cute seeing you blush for me. I saw you blush when you said I was pretty. I'm pretty, huh? And saying the play was made for me. An angel. Oh, Toni. You're so sweet."

"You are a star. And pretty, si. Bellissima. I swear it."

"*Your* star?"

"No, everyone's star. If you will be."

"Oh, Toni."

She pulled his shirt from his pants and ran her fingers across his stomach. Toni was overweight, but it made no difference. She liked the smell of his cologne and, more so, his touch. No, most so, *him.*

Her fingers glided along his stomach and up over his chest. Then they moved down, touching his belt. She opened the belt buckle, unfastened the button, and unzipped his pants. She felt him pull away, but she pressed her lips on his, tasting him again. Her palm ran along his cotton underwear, over his bulge. He moaned. That made her press more firmly, up and down, while making out with him. Then she yanked down his pants, reaching inside his underwear and touching his hard cock. She rubbed the skin while they continued to kiss each other's lips.

"Mina, oh Mina. But I … I don't think—"

"You don't want me to?"

"I … yeah, of course I do. But …"

Mina pulled his underwear down and held his cock in her hand.

She was surprising herself. Everything was happening so fast but, somehow, it had to. She knew Toni. If she didn't act quickly, she might never touch him again. He treated her like a little girl, despite always throwing stray glances of desire her way. She knew he had always liked her. And now … she liked him. He had made a play for her. *For her.*

She rubbed his shaft as he held her closer. He moaned again. His pants were on the floor now, while she tasted him, caressing his tongue and sucking his lips. She finally yanked his underwear all the way down his legs, while his hands ran over her body to the crack of her ass, pulling her closer to him as she continued to run her palm up and down his cock.

"God," he said between kisses. "Oh God, Mina. Mina."

He still sounded a little afraid, but his reticence drove her harder. She could hear him breathing heavily. She wanted him to breathe more heavily.

She wanted to take it in her mouth. Not his tongue—his cock. Inside. She felt the pleasure wetting her panties as she touched it.

She let him go for a moment and removed her robe. She wasn't wearing a bra, and his eyes widened at the sight of her boobs in the broad daylight of her apartment, but he couldn't enjoy the view for long as she pressed her chest against him, pushing him against the wall once more. Now, with just red silk panties and her naked bosom pressing against his chest, she kissed him over and over while still stroking him with her palm.

For a moment, she let go and pulled down her panties, letting them drop to her ankles. He looked down her body with wide eyes. She giggled and embraced him once more, pressing her naked skin against him. Then she grabbed his cock once more.

"Mina, wait. Maybe—"

"What?" she whispered, breathless. "What is it? You want me to stop?" she asked, stroking him.

"No, no, I don't … but—"

She felt something warm spill over her hand. The liquid trickled down her hand and dripped over her bare leg. It surprised her so much that she nervously laughed. As Mina backed away, he had a look of shame.

He leaned his forehead on hers. "I should go."

"It's okay, Toni. Forget it. I wanted this. Really—"

"No, no. I … I should go. I should go."

He quickly pulled up his pants, opened the door, and left.

PAINTING

MINA WOULD PAINT. SHE ALWAYS PAINTED WHEN SHE WAS upset. It made her happy. That's what she needed now. She wanted to be happy.

She wasn't happy.

What the hell was she doing? She had heard about producers blackmailing actresses for sex. She had been warned in school in Paris about that. But she had never heard of an actress offering sex *after* she was given the starring role. Why? Was she crazy?

Or did she actually like him?

She mixed a little water with the paint. Then she applied initial strokes. When she was in the mood, she could paint very fast. Today she was in the mood, so much so that she had barely prepared her workspace. It was like her bizarre sexual advance on her friend. She hadn't even bothered to properly place the mats on her floor. She'd just grabbed the paint and dove into the act.

Toni had given so much to her. And he was so sweet. And she adored his spirit. And he seemed to care so much for her. No one else cared for her. He had given her the starring role in his play.

Mina was a lonely girl. Her only real friends were Gail and Toni, come to think of it.

She painted. It took her mind off things—and the voice in her head. That odd French voice kept muttering, now coming so frequently that she did everything she could to ignore his words. She figured if she painted, she could ignore that too.

She first painted a frail man in a park. The day after her fall, she had walked the lovely Central Park Mall alone. The old man was an ice cream vendor selling cones by the side of the path, beside the benches, near a picturesque arch bridge. She enjoyed listening to him, he was so nice, as he scooped her some strawberry ice cream. She thought of trying to recreate all the wrinkles she had seen along his face and fore-head, his large nose, and his bushy white eyebrows, thin gray hair, and sparse beard. He had light-cerulean eyes. Really lovely blue eyes. She remembered that—cerulean, like the sky. The eyes were a bit sunken in. He was a thin man. Yes, she could paint him. She knew she could.

No. Her mood was somber.

You shall fall again.

"Shut up!" she snapped, looking all around her. "I don't want to hear you anymore. Stop talking. I can't take it anymore!"

She could paint clouds. The clouds had been thick. The gray above the New York skyline that afternoon had been beautiful in its own way.

No, she didn't want to paint scenery.

She started mixing paints and faced her blank slate.

I made love to you.

She shut her eyes, taking a deep breath. Erik, her phan-tom, sounded pained, or … jealous?

She started painting a child. She had watched a boy throwing a Frisbee to his dog while his mother read a book on a grassy hill.

No, that would turn into another poodle sketch. She had so many poodle paintings lying against the wall.

The canvas was taken off the easel and changed again. More words were heard and ignored. She thought he spoke in French.

She started sketching the people who she had watched sitting on blankets, picnicking, near the mother and boy beside the water. It had been nice and tranquil. But she didn't want to paint people either. She threw the brush down on the mat on the carpet in a huff and folded her arms.

How strange. She felt such an urge to paint, but she couldn't find a fucking thing to work on. Then she took a very deep breath and …

We made love last night.

"Fucking shut up! Damn you! Shut up! You're just a figment of my imagination … and I … I think I must be going crazy."

You're not crazy. I'm the phantom from the theater.

"Yeah? Why are you in my apartment, then?"

Why do you think you're crazy?

"You're speaking to me even though you don't exist. And … because I heard you talking when Toni was with me this morning, but he didn't hear you."

I don't want him to hear me. I only want to speak to you, Ms. Daaé.

"You were in my dreams. How is that?"

Then she felt a touch. It brushed against her neck and pulled down her suspenders. Then it ran across her breasts, along her hips, and down over her butt. Then it pressed where it was most pleasurable.

"Stop," she said, closing her eyes. "Stop it."

You don't want me to touch you again?

"No. I don't even know who you are."

I was an actor in your lover's play.

"My lover? He's not my lover. Toni's a friend."

That's not what I saw this morning.

"That's enough." She searched the room, wide-eyed in fear now. "Stop playing games with me."

She felt fingers gently touch her again. It tugged on her

hair, which she'd tied back in a bun, then ran along her ear and neck before caressing her chin. But then the touching stopped. It became quiet, with the exception of some murmuring from neighbors through the walls.

When the voice quieted, she started another painting.

She painted a group of people dancing around a fire. It was ancient man, dancing in some sort of mystic ritual frenzy. These men, dancing around the pyre, were half-clad in animal fur. She made the background twilight. She used orange and red along the horizon. Then she painted figures moving up and down to a beat that only she would ever know.

But it didn't take long for her to abandon this too. By the time she had worked on their faces, she was bored. And she felt like the figures were disjointed and not moving in unison. It was another failed piece of artwork.

Some painter she made. Maybe Toni was right. Maybe she was a better singer.

You sing like an angel.

She quickly changed the canvas yet again and brought up another blank slate. She stared for the longest time, sucking the tip of her brush and biting her nails. Meanwhile, she heard incessant chattering from her French ghost. She tried to do everything to ignore it or, at the very least, ignore what he was saying.

She painted with more fervor.

She gazed at her left hand as she painted with her right. Her naked hand would be her model. And she brushed fast, surprised at her vigor. She probably needed more nude model training to get the borders and angles perfect. She had painted subjects before but had always felt her education rather inadequate in regard to human anatomy. Nevertheless, she did her best at her self-portrait. And she didn't do a half bad job.

Her goal for this new piece was to bring out the three dimensions of the hand. Like her all-time favorite, the *Virgin of the Rocks* by Leonardo Da Vinci, she wanted the hand to appear as if it were reaching out to the viewer. This proved ambitious. And it took many efforts. But her hand furiously attacked the canvas.

After she was satisfied enough with the painting, she created an effect with color, particularly red, of paint dripping from the hand as if it were a melting hand of wax. It looked pretty good. When she had finished with the colors, her only regret was that it looked darker than she had intended. She wanted the hand to be dripping into obscurity, not appearing monstrous. But there was something frightening about the hand. Like all her paintings. Dark. Foreboding. All her work was like this.

She stared, while sucking on the brush, at her likeness of her own hand. Then she jumped as it started to move. At first, it turned. It fell perfectly still. Then it reached out to grab her.

Let me touch you!

"Stop it!" she screamed. "*Get out! Please leave me alone! Get out of here!*"

JUST A FRIEND

THERE WAS A KNOCK ON THE DOOR. SHE CLEANED HER HANDS on a towel and walked over. True to form, Gail was pressing her eye against the peephole while banging obnoxiously and laughing, jumping up and down.

"Hey, bitch," Gail said with a wave as Mina opened the door. "About time." Gail barged in as if the apartment were hers. She always did that when she visited. She meandered straight over to the refrigerator.

"Mina, I don't believe it. You have food."

"Not funny."

"But … where's your fucking beer?"

"Keep looking."

Mina regretted saying that. Gail started pushing stuff all over the place. Then she took containers out and stacked them on a countertop. Finally, she found what she was looking for. She had a bottle opener attached to her keychain. She opened two beers and gave Mina one with a large grin, as if Mina were *her* guest. Then she looked at Mina's clothes with distaste. Mina likely looked like a complete mess, wearing a long white frock covered with paint. Her hair was still tied back in a bun, and there was paint on her fingers and arms. Gail, on the other hand, looked very pretty in her white sleeveless T-shirt and black pants.

Gail jumped on the couch. "Whatcha doing?"

"Painting."

Gail raised the beer in a toast then squinted at her friend. "Hey, you wanna go with me and my gang tonight? We're clubbing. It's gonna be so much fun, Mina."

"I …" Mina bit her lip.

"What?"

"I just have to be ready for rehearsal. I promised Toni. Gail, if I don't go, I might be back working for Ms. Kuni again."

"She's so pissed. You should see her." Gail opened her big eyes wider and nodded. "She's using her fucking cat. Can you believe that? Everyone's drawing a fucking pussy. A real purring pussy, Mina. Not yours."

"Stop talking like that." But Mina couldn't help but laugh. "I told you, I don't like your trash talk."

"Just kidding. Actually, she's got some surfer boy who was in the class. Can you believe that? Anyway, a male's form is cute and all, but it's not like yours."

Mina wondered if it was the cute painter she'd ogled on her last morning there. He had a nice face and a hard body. He'd make a good model.

"Ms. Kuni's really pissed, Mina. You were such a great model. Poor teacher's not the same." Gail drank some beer to that. Then she smiled a playful smile at Mina.

"What?"

Gail shrugged, jumped up, and sauntered into the adjoining bedroom. Mina followed. Her failed paintings were all over the floor. Gail maneuvered around them and walked right up to the easel. Still sitting on a tarp was Mina's *Hand.*

"This one's good," Gail said after staring for a long time. "Wow!" She touched the frame. "Really good."

"You think?"

"Yeah. This is the best shit you've ever done. What … what is it?"

"What do you mean?"

"Well, I see it's a hand. What's it supposed to mean?"

"It's art. I don't know. Does it have to mean anything? It was more of a feeling than a scene."

"I fucking love it."

"Really?"

"Yeah. It's intense. I love it. It's like the hand is weeping, you know." Gail turned and gave Mina a very bright smile. "It's like anger. Rage. It's fucking intense. Reaching out. It's great."

"I'm glad you like it."

Gail laughed. Then she brushed her hand along Mina's arm. "Sometimes you talk so formally. It's cute."

"You know," Mina said, folding her arms and looking at her work, "I think good art, I mean really good art, doesn't always have to have a point, right, Gail? Sometimes it just *is*."

"Yeah. That's what's great about art. It's whatever it wants to be. It's not a thing. It just *is*."

Mina loved that. She nodded at Gail and realized that's what she loved about her. Gail was one of the few people who understood art. Like … Toni.

Gail turned and came right up to Mina's face. She seemed to search Mina's eyes.

It made her a little uncomfortable.

"This is anger, right?"

"Huh?"

"Anger? You're angry about something?"

"I guess."

"What? What are you angry about? The whole world's at your fingertips. I don't get it. Why are you mad?"

Mina nodded. She stepped back a little. "I don't know. I just don't know."

If Mina had the nerve, she'd have told her about the mishap with Toni. Of course, she'd never have told her about the voice. Or the moving hand. But she would have told her about her favorite clown. She really needed counsel, but she was shy.

Gail turned back to the painting. "It's fucking great, Mina. I mean it. It's you. It's fucking great. The best thing you've ever painted."

"Thanks."

"I guess …" Gail said. They both kept staring at it. A hand reaching out but dripping into obscurity. It was reaching out to them but disappearing. "It's kinda, horrific. It's like it's going away, right? Like the hand is disappearing. And yet, it's desperately trying to touch someone. Almost violently."

"For sure."

Gail smiled at her then looked back at the canvas. "It's your best work." Then she ran her fingertips along Mina's arm again. "So, what do you think? Can you go or not?"

"I really have to get up early tomorrow for rehearsal. Tonight's not a good night." But Gail nodded so smugly, as if this was just an excuse. For all Mina knew, this might be her last day off. "All right. Fine. As long as we're not back too late."

"Really? For real? Awesome!"

"We'll be back early? Like midnight, okay? You have to promise. I can't miss tomorrow. My friend will kill me."

Gail nodded. But then she lost her smile.

She walked really close to Mina's face again, as if examining her once more. Then she touched her shoulder, gliding her fingertips along Mina's shirt and against her skin. She looked up and stared into Mina's eyes. Then she leaned close with a smile, parted her lips, and tried to kiss her.

Mina abruptly pushed her away.

"I'm just fucking with you," Gail said with a giggle. "Can't wait to see you tonight."

Mina took a pin from her hair and started to quickly pick up her paintbrushes.

"Is it finished?" Gail sat down on a small purple beanbag

chair near Mina's bed. It was the only other furniture in the room. "Huh? Is it finished?"

"I don't know," Mina snapped. She ran the brushes along some paper and wrapped them in Saran wrap. Then she gathered up the mat under the easel. She liked the painting, so she wouldn't take it down yet, but she turned it away from the bed.

"What's the matter?" Gail asked. "Are you mad? I was just messing with you, Mina."

"Gail," Mina said, violently pushing paint into another bag. "I told you before. I'm your friend. And I like men."

"Geesh. I know." Gail leaned back and stretched out her arms on the beanbag chair with a bubbly smile. "Sorry … still, sometimes the wrong thing to do is … the funniest, right? Relax. You're so serious." Gail smiled widely, then she frowned at Mina's response. "Come on. You're acting like the world's about to end. I was just messing with you."

"Sure."

"I fucking love you, Mina. That's all. Just like your painting. I love that intense shit. It's just you. You're so quiet, but inside you're like ready to explode. I fucking love that. I'm with you. As long as I see you."

Mina leaned against the easel and faced her friend. Then she said sternly, "But are you?"

"Am I what?"

"Are you gay, Gail?"

Gail lifted an eyebrow and there was an uncomfortable silence.

With all of Mina's stress right now, that wasn't the response she was looking for.

Then Gail said, "I really need you tonight. That's why I came over. I need my *friend* at the bar. 'Kay? Get it? My *friend*. Can my *friend* join me?"

"All right. As long as you stop saying *fucking* and *bitch* and other trashy talk."

"Ooh, but I love it when *you* say it."

THE FALLEN ANGEL

A LITTLE AFTER TEN O'CLOCK, MINA SAT ALONE, GRIPPING A metal pole on the New York subway. She was on her way to the bar. She chuckled to herself about Gail's meeting time— so typical of her. A man across from her stood with his head dipped down, staring out a dark window. He looked homeless, with ragged clothes and disheveled hair, but he seemed oblivious to anyone, just staring. Closer to her, a young couple was pushing and pulling at one another, goofing off and laughing, with an occasional glance in her direction. But no one bothered her.

It was cold. Summer was over. She wore a white cotton sweater and clutched her arms close as she made her way up the tunnel escalator and across a seedy alley. Gail had told her that the Mole Hole was a new bar set in a basement. When Mina found a painted wooden sign with a mole hanging from a hole, holding a bottle, she knew she'd found the place.

The place was packed. There was a long line, but the bouncer let Mina pass the moment she arrived. She made her way down a very narrow and steep flight of stairs, shoulder to shoulder with strangers. It was crowded and dark, lit only by a handful of neon lights flashing red and green from the bottom of the stairs. And it was loud. Many shouted and hollered, but their voices were muffled behind the blaring thump of techno music.

Downstairs, the room extended almost like a warehouse with a bar, surrounded by bodies, at each end. Although it was cold outside, all the people dancing made it warm. She took her sweater off, wrapped it around her waist, and looked around. While gazing at a couple inappropriately grinding beside her, she was startled when someone yanked at her elbow.

"Haeey, hun!" said Gail. She staggered and smelled of alcohol as she kissed Mina's cheek.

Gail stumbled, and Mina had to catch her. Then they walked through swaying bodies to a raised table at the other side of the club.

"Cra-azy shit, eh, Mina!"

Sitting there on tall stools were Gail's friends. To her right were Lori and Raoul. She knew them from meeting with Gail in a restaurant a month ago. Lori was a dark-skinned girl with long hair. She wore a cute long-sleeved lime-green shirt and jeans. Raoul had on a preppy white button-down and brown slacks. They were Gail's best friend and Gail's brother. Raoul nodded, acting cool. Lori lifted her martini glass and smiled. Two girls Mina didn't know stood by the table, to her left, pointing and laughing at people while drinking from beer bottles. One of them nodded at Mina.

"Know my bro?" Gail asked, sliding Mina a beer bottle across the table.

"We met," Mina said, raising her beer bottle. "Hi again."

"Hi, Mina." Raoul nodded across the table. "Gail was talking about how you used to be together in class?"

Lori and Gail laughed. Raoul just furrowed his brow.

The two strangers beside the table laughed too, apparently in on Mina's former job. Lori leaned over and pointed at the two strangers. "That's Tiffany and Beatrice. Beatrice goes by Bee for short. This is Miss Mina Daaé, ladies."

The strangers nodded and went back to staring at dancers and gossiping. The two of them must have been close friends because they chose to wear nearly matching glittering rose skirts and kept talking between themselves.

Mina drank. She could barely hear a thing except the weird techno-heavy shit, thumping and pounding. It was pretty awful.

"How you doin'?" asked Lori, leaning over again and touching her arm.

"Great," Mina said with a smile. "Not as good as you guys, though. Seems I'm late to the party."

On cue, Gail closed her eyes tightly for a moment, dipped her head down, and quickly opened them. She looked up at Mina, smiled, and clumsily raised her beer. Lori laughed at her.

Mina turned to the couple grinding toward the center of the room. Everyone had made space around them and was clapping and cheering the couple on. It was a short bald guy, shirtless, with tattoos covering his arms and shoulders, abs cut as hell, a thin mustache, and blue jeans. He looked like a professional dancer and certainly moved like one.

"They're pretty good," Mina said, pointing. She turned back.

Gail wasn't looking at the dancers. She was smiling at Mina.

"How'd you find this place?" Mina asked Lori.

"I used to work here, when it was called the Rush. I bartend outside college."

"Really?" asked Mina. "I'd love it if you'd make me a drink one day."

"Oh, yeah? What's your taste, Mina?"

They had to talk loudly. Whether people were shouting, staring at the improvised entertainment, or jumping up and down senselessly to the thumping music, it was hard to hear.

"Beer," Mina said stupidly. "Oh … or margaritas. Martinis. I like sweet drinks."

Lori nodded with a kind smile.

"Sheez fuckin' good with mar—eenies," said Gail, nodding and cutting into the conversation. She spoke a little too loudly. "Try 'em. Made me a cosmo once, bitch."

"It wasn't that good, boo," said Lori, laughing.

"I'd love it if you made me one," Mina said. "What do you have there, Raoul?"

"Coke."

"L'il bro's underage," Gail said with a wink and a laugh. She put a finger to her lips and it sort of slid off her face. "We snuck him in."

"Where are you working now, Mina?" asked Lori.

"The theater."

"The *theater*," echoed Lori with her best British accent. "*The theater.* What are you doing at the *theater*, Miss Madam Mina?"

"I've got a part in a play," Mina answered with a laugh.

"*The Harryequin*," said Gail with a nod. "She's in *The Harryequin.*"

"*The Harlequin*," Mina corrected.

"Wow," said one of the two strangers leaning on the table. "*The Harlequin?* I've seen the posters in the subway. It's a really big play."

"Actually, she *is* the harryequin," Gail added, raising a finger.

The two friends stared at Mina. Then Gail caught everyone's attention as she started to tip over on her seat.

"Come, come, come bitch," Gail said, opening her eyes wider than normal. "Come with me to the bar. Let's see some other shit I can get you and me. Come on!"

"Sure you can manage?" Mina asked.

"Let's go!" Gail grabbed her by the arm and led her to one of the counters. She seemed to be using Mina more as a crutch than a companion.

The crowds along the bar were terrible. She wondered how Gail would get anything. But Gail fumbled her way through, tapping a shoulder or shoving between couples with a big smile. People made way for them and, somehow, they made it to the counter. She didn't have as much success with the bartender, though.

"I'm so glad you came, babe," Gail said in her ear.

"Thanks for inviting me. I think I needed a break before rehearsal."

Gail leaned over the counter, searching the bar. Two bartenders were really busy. "Fuck, Mina. We'll be here all night."

"You two care for a drink?" asked a tall, curly-haired young man leaning over the counter beside them. He was dressed sharply in a navy-blue suit, carrying two drinks in his hand.

"We're waitin' for 'em." Gail nodded and pointed at the bartender.

"You'll be waiting a long time. Here." He handed the two drinks to them.

"What's this?" Mina asked.

"You want a drink?" the stranger said. "Well, here you are. Got these for you."

They were purple and over crushed ice, in margarita glasses. The violet color looked weird. Gail didn't hesitate. She took her glass and started drinking it down.

"Umm," said Gail. "Not bad shit, Mina."

Mina hesitantly sipped hers. It had juice and some spices, with something alcoholic.

"Whas in it?" Gail asked. She had to tap on the man's shoulder to get his attention.

He was swaying to the music, acting all cool. He shrugged. Then the young man looked at Mina, top to bottom. "Where are you two from?"

Mina wasn't sure she liked this boy. He was alone. He didn't seem to have any friends, and yet he had this arrogance about him.

"Here," said Gail. She giggled. "How 'bout ya?" And she ran a single finger down his chest.

"Just visiting. I go to school in Georgetown."

"New York town?" asked Gail.

"He means Georgetown in DC, Gail," explained Mina with a laugh.

"Right," he said, raising a drink with a smile. "You've been there?"

"Yeah, I visited a friend going to school in DC once." Mina sipped more of her mystery drink.

"At Georgetown?" he asked.

"Um-hmm … This is good. What is it? Where'd you get it?"

"I don't know. I think they're mojitos. I just asked for something different. Purple. Wild, huh?"

"Yummmm," said Gail, practically hunching over. "Hey man, whas your mayor?"

"Political science."

Gail's eyes opened wide. "Reeeally? Come fuck o'er with us. You need to see my bro."

"Why, does he go to Georgetown?"

"No, he's one of your mayors."

"How much did your friend have to drink?" he asked Mina with a laugh.

Mina just shrugged. "How did you come across these drinks?"

"You shouldn't question gifts, my lady," he said with a smile and a wag of a finger. "Anyway, I was expecting two friends and got it for them. Seems I was stood up."

He acted nice. A little *too* nice. Mina didn't like that. She started looking at her drink with distaste. And why was the drink violet?

Gail gestured for him to follow them, but he put his hand up.

"Gotta use the bathroom," he said. "I'll be right back."

"How will you find us?" Mina asked.

"I'll look around."

Gail stumbled back into Mina's arms, nearly spilling the rest of the purple stuff all over Mina's shirt and white sweater as they went back to their table.

Mina leaned over and whispered into her ear, "Gail, why did you tell me to arrive late? I told you I had to be home early tonight."

Mina had been trying to summon the nerve ever since she first saw Gail drunk. Gail looked down and then seemed a little guilty.

"Don't worry 'bout it."

"Tell me," Mina insisted.

"Mina, I love you," Gail said with a guilty smile, flapping a hand over her arm. "I mean, I reeeally love you. But don't get me wrong. I just had to get them ready."

"Ready? Ready for what?"

Gail laughed.

Two drunken bastards fell right behind Mina, hurting her heel, and draped themselves over some bodies, laughing. That got them into a row with a few other bystanders and, for a moment, there was lots of shouting and pushing near them. A huge, burly bouncer came in the nick of time.

Gail almost fell over again. Mina grabbed her in her arms.

"What do you mean, *ready*?" Mina let Gail lean against her on their way back to their table.

"Mina," Gail said, with a slur, in her ear, "Mina, you know, baby, you're shy."

Then Gail pressed her lips against Mina's cheek. It was just a peck. But it bothered her. No, what Gail had said bothered her more.

So she was invited to come late in order to not … what? Bore her friends? Embarrass her? Jesus, was she that bad?

Mina felt warmth rush to her face. Gail was telling her that she was so awkward that her friends had to be drunk in order to be in her company. That was seriously fucked up.

And worse, Gail seemed very serious about it—even in her inebriated condition.

Mina tried not to spill Gail's drink. She had it in the same hand that held Gail as they made their way back to the table.

When she finally reached their stools, she felt angry. So mad that … no … she started … to feel dizzy. Really dizzy. Or was she just that upset? She really didn't feel that angry. So why was she dizzy? Was it the drink? She had only drunk one beer and this purple drink. She was swooning a little and, for a flash, returning to her spot at the table, Gail lost her smile and looked sick too. Had they been poisoned?

"What you got there?" asked Lori.

"*Mo-hee-tos!*" cried Gail, falling into Lori's arms.

"And you didn't get us any?" Lori added.

"Sorry," said Mina. "It's not as good as you could have made them."

"Let me try," said Lori. She took a swig of Mina's drink and shrugged. "Tastes a little sour. There's some…" She swished a little in her mouth. "Vodka. Maybe lemon. But I don't know what the other shit is. It looks like a Purple Rain."

Gail shrugged and burped.

Mina felt nauseous. And she hadn't liked the way that boy looked. He seemed too preppy and fake. She pushed her cocktail glass onto the table and grabbed her unfinished beer.

"So … what'd I miss?" asked Gail. Then she fell off the stool. Everybody burst into laughter. Gail raised a finger over the table.

"We were talking about football," said Raoul. "You like football, Mina?"

"No." Then Mina thought of what Gail had said about making sure she came late. "I mean … it's okay. It's okay, you know. I guess."

"I fucking hate football, bro," Gail said while being helped up by Lori. "I haaate football. And leave Mina the fuck alone." And Gail pinched her brother's cheeks.

Raoul just sat there and looked annoyed. Everybody laughed.

"I wonder if we can do pool?" asked Gail. She started searching the room. "I wonder. Is there a pool table here? Want to do that, Mina? Mina, you want to play pool with me, Mina?"

"If they have one," replied Lori, "people are dancing on it. Anyway, you really should just chill out."

And that's when it happened. Mina looked out at the people dancing, and she could have sworn their bodies were swaying like waves on the ocean. She rubbed her eyes. Her vision blurred. Her heart raced. She felt sweaty and terribly dizzy. For a moment, she thought she was going to throw up. Gail wasn't looking good either. But then again, Gail had an excuse, having probably drunk six drinks by now.

Mina closed her eyes. When she opened them, the swaying bodies looked normal again.

"I don't feel well," Mina admitted.

That seemed to alarm Gail. For the first time since seeing her friend, Gail seemed to become sober. "Are you okay, Mina?"

"I don't know. I just don't feel well. Maybe it was the drink."

Mina closed her eyes again. She was swaying on the stool.

"I don't feel great either," said Gail. Then she vomited all over the table, sending everyone reeling. But Gail was so drunk that she laughed, burrowing her head in her arms.

Raoul rushed over to Gail. Lori grabbed her over her shoulder and held her.

Then Lori cocked her head back at Mina. Lori became a blur.

"You okay, Mina?" someone asked.

"I think it's the drink."

"The Purple Rain?"

At that precise moment, a man tapped on Mina's shoulder. She figured it was the Georgetown stranger who had brought the drinks, and she intended to spin around and give him a piece of her mind, but it wasn't. It was a man dressed in a dark mask and cape. Erik. Her phantom. He looked ridiculously elegant surrounded by T-shirts and jeans in the nightclub. But he looked good. He always looked good.

When Mina turned back to her friends, they were still busy helping Gail and cleaning her mess.

Erik gently tapped on her shoulder again. Then he leaned beside her ear.

"Come join me, Miss Daaé," he said softly.

"Leave me alone, Erik."

"Join me," he whispered. "I'd like to show you something."

She shook her head.

"It's about your friend. You need to see this."

Mina turned, and he had a kind smile under his mask. He sort of faded in and out of focus and, for a moment, he even disappeared entirely. But his eyes, those striking jewels, came back into focus. They seemed kind. He touched her fingers with his soft white gloves—those lovely soft gloves.

"Come. Come with me."

Mina got up and followed, more out of curiosity than desire. She didn't even know how he was there. Or how people weren't staring at him in his dark nineteenth-century cape. People swayed around her and Erik as they seemed to pass them in slow motion under the bright swirling lights.

Somehow they made it to the center of the dance floor beside a bunch of kids jumping up and down like fools. He stood close to her and gently kissed her cheek. Then all the surrounding bodies seemed to slow. He gently rubbed her fingers with those soft gloves again. He turned her gently so she faced the strobing lights. Then he ran his gloved fingers along her long hair and they embraced, slow dancing. Mina would have thought everyone would be staring at them, but they didn't. They all kept pogoing along.

"I'm sorry if I gave you a fright," he said quietly in her

ear, "but I'm a ghost, my dear. I'm not always in control of how and when I appear."

And somehow that all made sense in his arms. And, as if proving it, his face blurred and for a moment she saw dancers jumping through him. But it didn't scare her. She felt at ease in his arms.

"Particularly with your psychic perception. Sometimes you pull me through at the wrong time. But I'm here now, Christine, so happy to be dancing with you. And not startling you."

She wasn't sure if he was referring to now or when the painting of her hand tried to grab her in her apartment. He gently brought her into a closer embrace.

"You did scare me, Erik," she admitted, nodding and leaning her head on his shoulder. "You did. Oh, Erik, I can't even be sure you're here now."

"But I am."

His cologne smelled nice. And she liked it when the bristles of his thin goatee ran against her cheek as he held her. Although everyone else jumped up and down with the hip-hop, she and Erik danced their slow dance. And it seemed lovely and felt right.

He kissed her on the lips.

"But why are you here, Erik? Why?"

She got lost for a moment in those lustrous eyes.

"Are you happy I'm here?" he asked in a whisper. His lips, half hidden under his mask, curled into a smile under the flashing light.

"Yes."

"Then that's all that matters. Follow me, Miss Daaé." He let go of her and took her hand again. "I want to show you so much more. Something about your friend."

They were off again, with him guiding her between bodies with his gloved hand, until they approached a wall beside a bar. Erik walked through the wall, reaching back for her. Only his gloved fingers were visible. That frightened her. Even though it was his soft white glove, having it emerge from the wall reminded her of her painting. It was so weird. Yet no one around them paid any notice.

"Come. Join me." And his white-gloved fingers reached for her again. "Come."

She gave him her hand and he helped her through the wall. She blinked and shaded her forehead with her free hand as a blinding yellow light shone over her eyes. It took a moment for her to adjust.

Her eyes focused on a grassy field and the sound of running water under the bright sun. There was bird song and a trickling brook near them. Her clothes had changed to a pitch-black dress. The sleeves were trimmed with frilly see-through lace ending near her fingers. Its long skirt extended down to a pair of glass slippers. She looked up at the clear blue sky, between branches, and realized that she was under a large leafless maple tree. Behind her was a forest of thorny maples, but in front of her was a steep, grassy hill. And at the top of the hill perched an elegant white medieval castle. The castle was perfect, without even the slightest blemish. It seemed to sparkle in the sunlight. Everything around her was bright and beautiful. And the air smelled fresh and clean. It was wonderful.

She walked by the side of the brook. Water trickled down a collection of jutting rocks and boulders, making a lovely waterfall. And thick, grassy moss clung to the rocks and boulders around the water. She stopped and looked down at her reflection in the water. She was surprised to see herself wearing a see-through veil, like a wedding veil, but black, pulled back behind her long, dark hair. She saw Erik's reflection beside her. His face in his shiny black half-mask, though handsome, looked a little disturbing standing over her. He leaned down and kissed her on the lips. They looked down at their reflections as they embraced. She closed her eyes and enjoyed the lovely sound of water as he entered her mouth again, dancing with her tongue. They embraced gently under the sound of bird song. Then he brushed her cheek with his white-gloved hand and gestured up to the castle.

"Come with me."

They walked hand in hand up the grassy knoll, Erik still in his black cape and mask and Mina in her matching ebony dress and veil.

There was a drawbridge over a shallow moat. They crossed creaky wooden planks over the bridge, and she heard music. It was a trance-like music, blaring from within the castle walls. It was as if they were approaching a house party, which was weird coming from such a lovely castle. Erik led her, holding her hand, until they reached giant wooden double doors.

"Welcome to his castle," Erik said with a smile and an exaggerated bow. It almost seemed like a joke.

"Erik, stop," she said, chuckling and pulling her hand from him. "What is this place? Where are you taking me?"

"The ruler's domain," he said, turning serious. "The king leads you to me. Our ruler. But the secret, Christine, is 'tis our kingdom. For he does not hold the courage that you and I hold. He is not willing to see what lies behind the mask. But if you join me, I will show you. Come and see."

She looked at him and those bright-green eyes behind the mask.

He smiled.

"I … I don't know where we are. Aren't we at the bar?"

He laughed. Then she laughed too, at the ridiculous sound of her question.

"This is the festival. Do you not care to meet the king?"

"Who?"

"Of course, you'll need a mask. Only certain guests are allowed. Are you a werewolf, vampire, angel, demon, witch, warlock, ghost, griffin, fae, fairy, nymph, mermaid, merman, satyr, mummy—"

"Out of all that," she replied with a laugh, "I suppose the closest would be an angel. I'd like to think so, anyway."

"An angel?" He nodded. "All right, that will do."

And Erik reached into the pocket of his long, dark cape and pulled out a black velvet mask. He handed it to her to wear over her eyes. "Here is your mask. Behind your back, your wings are folded."

"But what of you?"

"I am a phantom. Ghosts are always welcome at the gates."

"What is the place? Please tell me. Is this another dream?"

He furrowed his brow, and those green eyes stared for a moment. Then he pinched her arm.

"Oww!"

"Did you wake up?"

"No."

"Then it is not a dream. But are you sure you're an angel?"

She looked at him funny. "Yes. Yes, I'm very sure. I am an angel."

"Welcome in then, angel. Welcome, Christine the angel."

He opened one large wooden door and gestured for her to enter with a sweep of his hand. But as she entered, he remained standing by the threshold.

"Aren't you coming with me?"

He shook his head. "It's for you to know what's inside. Look at my mask. I already know."

Somehow, that made sense.

Mina walked through.

She found herself at the summit of a rocky ledge. She had to shield her eyes as the sandy valley below was so bright. Above the valley was a giant dome, blocking parts of the sky. The sides of the dome were made of turquoise stone. The center was a dusty glass dome. This dome was huge, towering very far above her. Directly below, along sand dunes, black stones moved like ants. She squinted and peered more closely, realizing that these black "rocks" were people. Thousands of dancers in dark leotards, covered in black paint, were moving on top of each other over a field of sand dunes. The black paint, like tar, dripped down their faces and hair, and they smeared it about their bodies and the bodies of their partners. The chaos was such a huge contrast to the quiet forest and grassy fields outside the palace walls. And the music blared in step with the chaos.

Mina looked back at the doors but Erik was gone.

A small man crouched beside her, hunched into a ball, with onyx paint upon his face. He had a violet lyre on his lap, but he didn't play. The hypnotic music blared. Then a violet light was cast over the small man's face, almost like a purple floodlight. She jumped back, seeing him open more than two eyes. He had rows of eyes along his face. Then he pointed down the ledge with a very sharp stump of an arm.

"Enter, Mina the angel."

The man stood on eight legs and scurried quickly, like a giant spider, down a dirt trail by the right side of the sandy ledge.

Among the dancers covered in black paint, down the valley, was a motley crew of circus freaks: jugglers, pipers, green-skinned witches, knights, kings and queens, acrobats, puppeteers, tightrope walkers, children in brown tatters, and mimes. Some of them were trapped in a rocky wall, with half their bodies emerging from the walls. Their chins rested on the backs of their hands. They appeared to be deep in thought, reminding her of that famous statue, *The Thinker*.

And then came the Harlequin. A man dressed in thick, white frills making his way, weaving this way and that, in the pandemonium. Bucking and jumping, he danced toward a central wooden stage on the opposite side of the valley. On stage, naked men and women contorted and twirled like ballerinas, spinning about and carrying streamers of all the colors of the rainbow. So many naked bodies, some white as sand or black as obsidian, dancing or fucking on the large stage above the tar dancers in the valley below. As the fluffy white clown made his way through the tar-dripping dancers, they ran their fingers and palms over his face, along the sides of his body, and over and under him.

"May I introduce an angel," someone announced.

Three more black spiders with large torsos and eight pointy spidery stumps crept beside her. Multiple eyes alternated from open to shut. She didn't flinch. Standing wide-eyed and frozen, she was too shocked at the nonsensicalness of it all to move. There was a sandy path, to her right, that led down the incline and to the central stage. Something drove her to go there—to visit her clown? She wasn't sure. But as she heard the tapping of eight more legs and a shadow passed over her, she decided that she'd fare better among the dunes of tar-drenched bodies than up on the cliffside with arachnids.

As she made her way down the dirt trail, mimes with part of their bodies trapped in the dirt walls gestured for her attention, life-size marionettes dropped down from wires hanging from high atop the glass-dome ceiling, and merchants, artists, and shopkeepers by tents along the walls just stared at her.

There was art on the walls. Beautiful paintings and sculptures fixed to the dirt walls mixed with vibrant green vines and carmine and lavender rose petals. It was elegant and regal, and ... colorful. She loved to look upon the earthen walls as she ventured down among the dancers.

Soon she was in the middle of the hornet's nest. Close to the dancing figures, she found that there was more space to navigate around them than it had seemed from the summit. She walked down dirt steps, dodging a group of contorting bodies. Some smiled, but most ignored her. Then a couple of them stopped spinning and grabbed her hands, helping her make her way faster to the stage across the valley. She didn't like the feel of their wet, blackened hands, and some of their tar adhered to her fingers.

By the time she was helped up steps to the stage, the Harlequin was sitting on an elevated throne, looking past the squirming nude bodies to look at her. She recognized this harlequin. He was fatter than Toni, but he had the same short black hair, ruddy nose, and hazel-brown eyes. Yes, behind the clown face, the man behind the mask was not just a harlequin. It was Antonio Vollini. But a big Antonio, so large that he could barely move from his throne.

"May I present Mina Daaé the angel," someone announced.

Toni looked down, seeming to recognize her. He lifted a glass of wine and toasted to her. "Si, si. But this is a fallen angel, no?"

Then, as quickly as it had begun, the sound of the dancers stopped. The naked bodies fornicating at her feet faded. The arena emptied. It was just her and Toni.

Mina looked at Toni's face and recoiled in fear. He was contorted in pain. He leaned against the side of the throne as bright red oozed from the folds of his white puffy clothes. His face winced behind the painted frown. There was a gurgling sound. And then he cried out, like that terrible cry he had uttered during the fall in her dream. He suffered as his white chest and legs were coated in crimson.

Mina turned to run, but she couldn't. Something pulled at her to stay.

When she looked at him again, it only became worse. What was once a frilly white clown was now a red-dripping wad of flesh. He attempted to stand, but he was too big. Then she watched as pails of red liquid were thrown over him from behind. This liquid was the same blood color as his now-drenched suit. It hit his face, turning his makeup from white to crimson. And as the blood splashed across his face, he seemed to suffer more, unable to avert the deluge. Mina ran as hard as she could back up the dirt trail.

Red rained down from the rafters of the glass-dome ceiling. It began as a drizzle of blood spotting the sand. Then it became a downpour. She was desperate to not be covered by it. It was as if it were poison.

She had to get away, but she couldn't. Her lacy black dress was soaked now, just like the Harlequin's white suit. Then she looked up, and what seemed like bucketfuls of blood fell over her face, her hands, and her head. She threw the wet veil over her head, but this only splashed more blood on her hair and face.

"*GET IT OFF ME!*" she screamed. "*GET IT OFF! OFF!*"

She turned back. Her "king" was no longer recognizable. Toni had become a mass of bloody gelatinous pulp, bubbling on center stage.

"*Get it off me!*"

Then she saw a spider with tar dripping from his face. He crept toward Mina on eight long, spider-like legs, removed a mirror from behind his body, and gestured for her to look at the mirror. Mina's face was covered in blood. It was so red that she could barely recognize herself.

"*GET IT OFF! OFF ME!*"

OFF

"Get off me!"

"Mina, I'm trying to help you!"

"*Get off!*"

"Are you okay?"

"Get off me!"

"Wake up, Mina. Come on! Wake up."

"Huh?" She sleepily cracked open an eye. Gail was leaning over her. Mina shook and looked around. She found herself lying on a couch. She saw a dimly lit room and the night-light from a kitchen—her kitchen. Then she looked at the beige cloth of her couch. She was home.

"Morning, crazy," Gail said, her voice bubbly. "Hi."

Mina felt dizzy. Gail fell out of focus and the couch seemed to move. Even the ceiling swayed. She turned to the floor and threw up beside the couch. Gail had been ready and pushed her head close to a bucket. It helped. She felt a little better. But she still felt terribly sleepy.

"That was a good idea."

"It wasn't the first time. You've been throwing up for hours. Made me sick just watching you. And you've been talking all kinds of weird shit, in different languages. It's been really scaring me. You're totally fucked up like me, bitch, which … I really don't get. You had like two drinks. Did you drink before you came?"

"No. I think I was drugged."

"We had the same drinks," Gail said, shaking her head. "I had a lot of them."

"Maybe roofied. Or like PCP or something? That guy looked really suspicious, Gail."

"You're crazy." Gail shook her head with a laugh. "You just drank too much. Maybe you're not used to it. I don't know. Or maybe he spiked yours with too much vodka."

"That guy from Georgetown looked suspicious."

"Yeah? Well, he was worried about you when you drifted off. He was helping Raoul and Lori get you into the car—along with me."

Had she passed out and had it all been a nightmare? It must have been a long time. Gail was barely slurring her words now.

Mina tried to sit up but felt too weak. Then she gazed at her clothes. Her dress and veil had disappeared. For a moment, she had been terrified that she would be dressed in a black gown, lying beside a dead tree or something. The dream had been so real. But she was wearing her red silk robe instead.

"You changed me?"

"Yeah. You vomited all over your clothes."

"Shit."

"It can be washed," Gail said, with a chuckle and a yawn, touching her arm. "Relax."

Relaxation was one thing Mina could do. In some ways, that was the thing that made her so nervous. Not only did she feel numb, but she felt so tired that she could barely move her arms or legs. She felt like she was above her body. Almost as if she were floating as Gail crouched over her.

"What's … wrong with me?"

"Rest." She shrugged. Then she ran a hand along Mina's bangs. "You're home. Maybe you should sleep."

"What time is it?"

"Around ten."

"Ten!" Mina jumped up. Gail quickly grabbed her wrist, but Mina wasn't up for long as the walls swayed. And now she noticed daylight from the kitchen window and through drapes in her bedroom.

"Ten?" she asked. "Why is it day outside and—"

"Ten in the morning."

"Huh?"

"Mina, relax," Gail said, chuckling, grabbing her. "Come on. Just stop. It's okay."

"But the play! Fuck. I promised Toni, Gail. Oh God, he's going to kill me."

"I spoke to him. Don't worry. When he saw you, he said he'd be back in the afternoon to pick you up. Just rest. It's okay. He said you could miss the morning rehearsal."

Mina squinted at Gail. She still wore a white cardigan, sports bra, and jeans. Her long golden hair was disheveled. She hadn't even changed her clothes since the bar.

Mina laughed.

"What's so funny?" asked Gail with a smile.

"You look like shit too."

"Hey, thanks." Gail fell back on the couch, bringing Mina into her arms. "I feel like shit. My head is splitting. But I'm all right. When I'm with you." Gail held her, stroking her hair.

Mina closed her eyes.

"Let's just go to sleep together again."

But a little later, Gail asked her quietly beside her ear, "Do you like me, Mina?"

"Huh? What do you mean?"

"I mean, I feel so incredible when I'm around you. I fucking love you. But I'm so fucking lonely. Last night was amazing. My bro and Lori are nice, but Lori's distant. And I don't see much of her anymore. Anyway, I don't feel the same way I do when I'm with you. I don't feel the same way with anybody."

"Then why'd you invite me so late to the bar?" Mina surprised herself at the edge in her voice.

"I had already promised to meet her stuck-up friends."

"They didn't seem so bad."

"They're Lori's peeps." She felt Gail shrug. "I don't mind getting plastered with them, but that's it. With enough liquor, Tiff and Bee lighten up. Without drinking, they're just bitches who set you up through a barrage of fucked-up questions. I didn't want them to do that to you. They were already saying stupid things about your model job."

Mina nodded and closed her eyes again. She felt so tired.

"Yeah, I like you, Gail."

Gail kissed her cheek and hugged her close again with a giggle. "Me too. Feeling better?"

Mina nodded. Soon her friend's rhythmic breathing helped soothe her.

Later, she didn't know when, Gail leaned over and pecked Mina on the cheek. Mina could smell the alcohol still on her breath. Then Gail touched her lips to hers. Mina opened her eyes. Gail smiled, looking right at her. Then she leaned back into the couch, closed her eyes, and clutched Mina close again. Mina thought nothing of it. She drifted off again.

Still later, she heard a giggle. She felt fingers glide along her chest under the soft robe, exploring her breast and nipple. And then another hand moved the robe back and ran along her leg. Mina gently pushed her hand away, but Gail seemed persistent, continuing to touch her breast with the other hand. Then Gail changed position, moving on top of her. She kissed her lips again. "Mmm." Gail sucked Mina's lip and entered with her tongue, kissing more passionately while gliding her fingers along Mina's belly button. "That's nice." Then a hand ran down to her legs again, sliding under her underwear.

Mina opened her eyes wide and then ... threw Gail off the couch.

"I like men!"

It wasn't the first time a girl had touched her. She had met a girl in high school who liked her too. But this was different. Gail was her best friend.

"Sorry," Gail said, stretching an arm on the carpet, laughing nervously. "Geesh. Couldn't resist. Anyway, it's no different from how you touched me in your ramblings earlier."

I did?

Gail jumped up and laughed. "Phony," Gail accused, flashing her a big grin.

"I like men," Mina said again. But she felt so tired saying it. She leaned back in the couch.

"Well, I like you," Gail said with a shrug, cocking her head back. "Perhaps later."

Then, with her back to Mina, in the light of the morning sun streaming through the drapes, Gail removed her sweater and sports bra, pulled down her jeans and panties, and stood naked for a moment. Her blonde hair was disheveled. She stretched her arms high with a yawn, tightening the crack of her ass, and ran a hand down the side of her breast, silhouetted in the light from the kitchen window.

Her standing like that there nude, on display, was seductive. But before Mina could say anything, Gail cocked her head back with another yawn, giggled, and said, "Excuse me. Gotta shower. I can only hold you for so long, bitch. And these clothes smell."

Mina closed her eyes. She heard the shower turn on.

Her friend Gail was gay? This in and of itself was not a problem. But she had the hots for her? That could be a problem for their friendship.

Gail had said she had touched her. She didn't remember that. To be honest, Gail was attractive, but Mina had never instigated touching another girl, unless she touched Gail last night? It was another piece of this mysterious nightmare. The whole evening scared her. She felt so confused.

After a long time spent staring at the dim light of the kitchen, Mina heard the water turn off. Then she heard her friend's bare feet walking toward her. Mina looked up and Gail stood in front of her again, her naked body now dripping wet. She ran the towel over her chest, drying her breasts, and then along her sides. Then she just held the towel by her side and stood there for a moment, looking deeply into Mina's eyes.

"I have a confession to make," Gail said terribly earnestly. She dried her ears and ran the towel up over her hair. "Maybe it's the beer—well, at least being drunk has given me the nerve to finally tell you—but, Mina, I've had the hots for you. I've been attracted to you ever since you first posed for class. It's not just that you're a drop-dead gorgeous model, or how fucking amazingly nice a friend you are. I'm really into you. And God, your body is, like, so incredible. Like really hot."

Gail reached out her hand and Mina took it, gently lying Gail back onto the couch beside her.

"And you want to fuck me," Mina said softly with a chuckle, putting an arm around her.

"Yeah," Gail replied too seriously, cocking her head back. "Yes, I do. I want to fuck you, Mina. Really badly, actually."

THE HANGOVER

Mina woke to a pounding in her head—or was it a pounding on her front door?

She squinted and recognized her kitchen and living room. She was lying in her red robe on her couch again. Then she heard the door open and Gail's voice.

"Huh?" asked Gail with a yawn. "Yeah, what? What is it?"

"Is she better?"

Mina recognized an Italian accent. Toni. She turned and saw him standing by her front door in jeans, a striped button-down shirt, and loafers. True to form, he turned to her and nodded. Mina groaned, rubbing her head.

"Mina, it's time," Toni said with a smile. "We've gotta go." He walked over and crouched beside the couch, touching her arm. "I'm not letting you play hooky anymore. You promised, yeah?"

Mina nodded.

"She's still not feeling well," Gail said, brushing her long blonde hair back and hanging by the door.

"No matter," Toni said, raising a finger. Then he gave his

infamous grin to Mina. "It's time. I have my driver waiting. You promised."

"Sure, Toni," Mina groaned. "Sure." Then she sat up. The whole room spun for a second. "Shit, Gail, I knew I shouldn't have gone."

"She's still sick?" Toni asked Gail.

"Too much fun last night," Gail said with a shrug and a giggle. Then she walked into the kitchen. Mina noticed Gail was wearing the matching red robe from her closet. "Before you guys go, I'll brew up a quick brew, babe. 'Kay? It's my special concoction made to end all hangovers. Trust me."

"What's in it?" Mina asked, sitting up and holding her head.

"Aspirin and chamomile with a dash of honey."

Mina laughed. Then she rubbed her forehead again.

"Mina, I left your clothes on the bed next to mine," Gail said from the kitchen. "I remembered your rehearsal. You better go now."

Mina shuffled off the couch and hunched over it for a moment. Finally, she forced herself up to make it to her bedroom.

The thin red curtain, only partly open, let in the bright light of the morning. The white sheets were wrinkled and all over the place, half hanging off the mattress.

Though her bedroom was small, a door demarcated it from the rest of the studio apartment. So she closed her door and got dressed.

She didn't hear a word from Gail or Toni. She pictured Toni pacing and looking at his cell phone and Gail ignoring him. His smiles didn't hide his true feelings. Mina knew full well he was pissed.

The room spun as she put her pants on and, although she prided herself on her balance as a dancer, she fell over onto the mattress when lifting her other leg.

Shit, I think I'm going to throw up again. How can I go to rehearsal?

You have to, Mina, for Toni.

When Mina opened the door, indeed, a very agitated Toni was sitting on the couch, staring at his phone. Gail ran over with a giggle and handed Mina a paper cup of her hangover tea. It smelled awful. She didn't want to eat or drink anything.

"I'll have it on my way."

Gail nodded, hugged Mina, and kissed her cheek. Then she hugged her again—a little too tightly—chuckled, ran a finger along Mina's bangs, and whispered in her ear, "It was fun last night. *A lot* of fun."

"Close up the apartment, will you?"

"For sure."

On the car ride, Toni stayed quiet—weirdly quiet. He just looked out the window as they drove through downtown, periodically checking his phone. But he forced a smile whenever Mina looked over.

Mina felt her bowels turning. Would she make it to the theater without having to use the bathroom? Just like at her audition, she began thinking about her abilities—how she was inferior to the professional dancers, how her voice was unpracticed, how she couldn't live up to Toni's expectations. And then she thought of the pedestal. Would she fall again?

You will fall.

"Shut up!" Mina snapped.

Toni jerked and turned. "Che?"

"Nothing." She looked down and rubbed her head. "Shit." Then she turned to Toni. "Not you, I was just thinking … out loud. Sorry."

"You've been doing that a lot lately." Toni nodded and patted her hand.

"I'm so sorry, Toni."

Toni shrugged. Then he turned back to the window.

A quiet Toni was worse than a loud one. He was too frenetic a man for silence to be normal. After Mina had waited long enough for a response and was about to turn back to her window, Toni laid a finger on his cheek and said, "This Gail … this Gail of yours, she's a good friend, no?"

"Yes. I met her at the university. She's a student."

"From your art class?"

"Yes."

He didn't like that. It seemed he had thrown the suggestion out, hoping she'd say no. "She seems to like you."

"She's a really nice girl. She's got so much energy. She's young."

"That's what I think of you," he said with a tight grin and a nod.

"I don't have a lot of energy," Mina said with a chuckle. "And I'm not all that much younger than you."

"Twenty years."

She shrugged.

Then they went back to looking out their respective windows. And Mina thought of Toni's patience. How could he wait the whole morning for her? The director must have been livid. Toni must really want her in the play to be this patient.

"I'm sorry," Mina repeated. "I really am."

Toni nodded. Then he turned to her with a fake grin and said, "Tell me … is this Gail gay?"

The car stopped at a red light just at that moment. The same moment Mina froze. She furrowed her brow. Then a car beside her window honked and made her jump. But it probably wasn't the car that had startled her.

They say that a woman possesses a special intuition. Well, right now it seemed Toni did. Had they been that obvious?

"I … I don't know," Mina replied.

"I'm very in tune with this sort of thing, you know. I'm also very observant. I like to think that's what makes me a good writer and producer." Then he nodded. "Don't worry. If she is gay, I don't mind. I have nothing against lesbians, of course. I suppose it's—"

"Then why are you asking?"

He nodded in thought and turned back to the window pensively. For some reason, his silence made her angrier. It would have been better if he had shouted at her. But she had never seen Toni get mad. She didn't even know if it was possible.

But Mina got mad—very easily.

"What happened between us happened," she snapped.

"Che?" He turned to her and almost tried to force a grin. "Between you … and I? Or Gail and …"

"Between you and me. What happened in my apartment, happened, Toni. And it's okay. I'm okay with it."

"I wasn't going to even mention that."

"Well, it happened. Okay?"

Toni nodded.

"And what else happens in my apartment, with other people, is my business. Not yours. You might be…" Mina looked at the driver. He was playing music softly—some sort of hip-hop—and he looked like he had no idea what they were talking about. But it didn't feel private. "You might be my producer, but what I do outside the play is really none of your business."

"I know." Then he turned and gave her his famous smile, but somehow it looked very fake this time. "Sorry if you thought otherwise."

She nodded. Then Toni turned morosely back to the window, and Mina felt awful.

"Oh, I'm sorry, Toni," Mina said, touching his hand. "Forget it. And … thanks for being so patient with me for your play. I don't know how you could wait so long for me."

"*You* are my play, Mina. I told you that. Are you feeling better?"

"Yes. I suppose."

"I am so glad."

"I won't do it again."

Won't do what again, Mina? Fuck Gail?

Really, if Mina was to be honest with herself, she had more problems with what had happened than Toni did.

Why did she touch Gail? What was she thinking? She had never slept with a woman before. Was it the alcohol? How? She'd had less than two drinks! And her nightmare. But she had been awake. Had she been awake?

You're losing it, Mina. You need to see a psychiatrist. And this isn't your phantom talking—it's YOU, your conscious mind. Your conscious mind mulling over the fact that yes, Mina, YOU DID, IN FACT, FUCK Gail last night. WHY!? Maybe you are gay?

She started crying. She couldn't believe it, but tears were running down her face and she shook a little. She did her best to turn and hide it from Toni, leaning toward the window. Then she gulped hard, straightening her body and using all the strength she had to stop. She didn't want to fall apart. Not in front of Toni. Not after everything this man had done for her. The last thing she wanted was for him to comfort her. And how could he?

But she knew she was crying for him because she felt like she had hurt him.

Or maybe I like Toni?

She glanced over, but he was still staring out the window. If he had noticed her crying, he wasn't admitting to it.

She forced down some of the tea in the cup she'd brought. Then she thought again how strange it was that she had a hangover at all. It must have been that suspicious man who gave her the purple drink. He must have poisoned her.

No one poisoned you last night, Christine.

THE REHEARSAL

For Mina, a girl who was pathologically shy, the crowd hanging around the stage to greet her that afternoon—literally a frenzied circus—was overwhelming. But she liked the attention. She had so many things on her mind and she needed distractions. It was the oddest motley crew she had ever seen. Only Toni could mix such extremes of art.

Two strongmen, as wide as Mina was high, stood by the end of the stage. Their long, thin, Salvador Dalí–like beards draped down over their lips. Jugglers dressed in clown face laughed and threw all sorts of trinkets into the air. One hurled a rainbow scarf at Mina's face. Acrobats ran and flipped over one another. There were singers practicing single notes over and over again. A man on stilts, in a suit—with a way-too-wide smile painted on his face—walked to and fro across the stage. And there were animals. A cage of birds and a young man, in jeans and a T-shirt, sitting beside a metal cage big enough for a lion. But there wasn't any lion—none that Mina could see or hear anyway. All the while, ballet dancers in tutus turned on their tippy-toes, practicing their routines in any space they could find. And gymnasts walked on their hands or landed in somersaults.

But the "normal" ones were just as fun. The "normal" ones hugged and kissed Mina, their star, on the cheek, shaking her hand or offering to meet for a drink at break time. They were all overly smiley, as if they had known her all her life. And all thrilled to see their main performer, Mina Daaé, sing again. Some might have been in suits, but they were ar-*tists*, just as looney as the bohemians. They reminded her of all her roommates and friends at art school in Paris. She loved them. They scooped her in their arms and acted as if she were their long-lost best friend. And as they embraced her, she caught Toni in the background, flashing a warm side glance. Finally, a genuine Toni smile. He knew theater was her home. And she supposed, from his grin, that he also knew that it was *his* show making her dreams come true.

It went on like this for half an hour, until Toni's claps echoed through the hall. He was clapping as loudly as he could at the center of the stage.

"Get to your places, everyone," he shouted. "You see her. Now the break's over. It's time to practice."

"Till later, Mina," said a dancer with a wink. Dressed in a light-blue pancake tutu, she looked like a dancer in *Swan Lake*. "Promise?"

"Don't forget to text me the link to your paintings," said a young man in glasses, a hoodie, and slacks.

Toni clapped some more.

When enough space had cleared, Mina spotted Daniella, dressed in a navy-blue suit and high heels. She and a gentleman were walking toward Mina and Toni, from stage left, and binders were tucked under her arm. The man walking beside her also had papers in his hands. This guy was a short, bald man in his thirties, who seemed to be taking in everything around him.

"Hi, Mina," said Daniella. "Let me introduce you to Henson Jenny. Our director."

"Mina," Henson said, sticking a hand out.

Mina shook his hand.

"Wait till you hear her voice," said Toni with a gaping smile.

"I'm more interested in seeing her dance," said Daniella. Then she examined Mina head to toe. "You'll need to practice. You're mine after rehearsal from five to seven every day. Got me?"

Mina nodded.

"She won't disappoint," Toni said.

The raucousness only increased. Toni looked around, annoyed. "I don't know what to do with these people."

Henson looked around too. Mina jumped when he shouted, "*Get the fuck out! Unless you're up! Get out!* Now that she's here, we're starting from the beginning. And if you're not in the first act, then … fuck! What are you doing here?"

And they obeyed. Toni looked at his director and shook his head.

Henson smiled smugly.

"You need to change, Mina," Henson said, his demeanor completely changed, almost sweet. "You don't come in until later. I'm sorry I missed hearing you sing at the audition. From what I hear, you were incredible. Let's do that again opening night, shall we?"

Mina nodded.

On a stool before a huge vanity mirror in her dressing room, Mina stared at herself. She took deep breaths. She was wearing a red silk bra and matching panties, sitting beside a glittering, puffy scarlet dress, trimmed in gold, hanging over a chair. She didn't have to apply makeup; it was a rehearsal. But she did want to brush her hair and look more presentable, rehearsal or not.

The dressing room was full of pomp. It was the most prized dressing room in the theater. And it was huge, with a lounge with a TV and sofa. Chairs surrounded the green leather couch, adorned with expensive mauve and cherry-red suede pillows. Elegant lamps surrounded the sofa. Thick gold coils framed a sign reading *The Harlequin*. Even the door was of a finer, darker wood than everybody else's. The room was gaudy and ridiculous. It was "Toni." And she figured that was why he had been so excited to show her this dressing room when she had first arrived.

The stark change from the production crew crowding around her to the peace and quiet in her dressing room was a little unsettling. Only a few dancers had nodded at her as she had walked down the dark hallway. Now it was completely silent, though she knew that, above her, the orchestra was playing and the dancers and jugglers were performing.

She sat like this for a while, just gathering her thoughts. Her dizziness had lifted. Now she was just plain nervous.

In the mirror, she noticed a shadow among the boxes and hangers and an old costume in the far side of her room. At first, she thought nothing of it, for it was still. But then something shifted in the darkness. She spotted the form of a body. Looking closer, she saw that the figure wore a black cape and a familiar black half-mask. It was Erik, sitting on a stool, hands folded, staring at her. Erik. Her phantom.

She whirled around and quickly drew her hands over her chest and waist. "I'm not dressed!"

"I've seen it before," the man quipped in his French accent. He chuckled. "Anyway, this is my dressing room, fallen angel."

He was so still and quiet that she could almost believe he hadn't said anything. He seemed to blend in with the shadows.

"I'm not dressed," she said again, jumping up and pointing to the door. "Get out of here."

He turned from her. "Go ahead, put on your costume. I'll turn. Wear it if he must humiliate you like he humiliated me. It only brings you closer to your fall."

Mina's heart was racing. She slowly leaned back in her chair, but she didn't dare take her eyes off him.

"I said leave. I'm—"

"Not dressed? Oui. I told you, I saw more than that in your forest."

"What forest? I don't know what you're talking about."

"Faker. I call you that." And he raised a finger. "You are a faker, an actor, and a good one but … not a liar. A faker. My mademoiselle, Christine Daaé, could never lie. You're too sweet an angel to lie. But fake you will. You will fake. And you will fake all the way until your end, won't you, Christine?"

Mina reached over to the other stool facing the mirrors and grabbed her huge frilly dress, because there was no way she was going to make a run for it half naked. The creep was right next to the door. She stood up and started pulling the dress on, but she didn't stop glancing at him.

He actually looked bored. He kept his hands folded and gave a few sighs.

"You can't be here," she said with a nervous laugh. "Not in my dressing room. You don't exist."

"The dressing room is mine, ma chérie."

"Why?" She straightened her red dress over her shoulders. It was so heavy she had to strain to lift it. Thankfully, it was to be worn only for a short while at the very end of the first act. It weighed down her shoulders. "This is my dressing room. I've been given the starring role."

"No, this is my dressing room. It says 'The Harlequin' outside the door, does it not? And I was given the starring role in Paris when you weren't even out of school yet. You know, you're a careful bird, but you're a little too trusting of Toni. Sure, your fuck-clown has a painted smile, but sometimes the nicest of clowns are the most vicious. Did you look up Monsieur Antonio Vollini's record in Europe? Did you check his show? Did you surf the web and look up what it was about before the circus came to town? Or did you just sign up like an imbecile? Stupide like me?"

Mina didn't answer. After all, he was just a figment of her imagination. She never saw him across the stage when she fell.

Nor did he ever show her that nightmare castle. And if all of it had been a figment of her imagination then, certainly, he was a figment of her imagination now. He was a hallucination. He wasn't real and he wasn't here. So she ignored him.

No, I am here.

"*Goddammit!*" Mina put her hands to her ears.

She faced him again. He was motionless, which seemed creepier. And this time, he stared with glowing green eyes behind that shiny mask.

She turned back to the mirror and leaned her head in her hands. "Why do you keep haunting me?"

"Am I frightening you? Oh, but I must. I must. When it's showtime, do not play the role. No. Let Antonio play it. Let him kill himself, not his lovers. That was his intention. His plan was to be the Harlequin if you didn't reprise the role. That would have been better. I would much rather throw Toni to his death than you. You're too nice."

Mina picked up her scarlet hat. It was a ridiculous, huge, feather hat.

"You're not actually going to wear that?" he asked with a laugh. "Really? A fucking burlesque hat? Why not go naked? Reprise your modeling role."

Mina refused to respond. She simply readjusted the tall, feathery hat.

"Quit, Christine. Don't go on. Let him wear that and make a fool of himself. Don't strut your tits and ass and dance for a fuck-clown. I showed you the valley. I showed you who he really is. Do you wish to be like him? Let him be his own peacock."

"Why do you care about me?" Mina asked, spinning around again. "You—"

He was gone.

"Oh, my God," she said to herself, raising her hand to her mouth.

She found it difficult to breathe. She felt trapped. She took a deep breath and looked at herself in the mirror—while doing everything she could to keep her eyes off the shadowy corner of the room. Her face was white as a ghost.

She jumped from a loud knock on the door.

"You're almost on, Mina." It was Vince. "We're all waiting for you. You doing okay with that heavy dress?"

"Yeah. I'll be right out, Vince."

THE SCARLET DRESS

Henson Jenny might not have made her apply makeup, but her dress was so thick, heavy, and ridiculous that she would have preferred to hide behind clown face. Everyone turned, and it wasn't just because she had the starring role this time. She wore the bright, puffy, gilded scarlet dress with a matching red train that ran fifty feet behind her. In fact, she had to wait about fifteen minutes just for the crew to hang more frilly cloth along the sides, properly attach the tail, and be ready to follow her out onto the stage. The train was carried by stagehands dressed in red and black camouflage meant to blend in with the shadows. And it seemed, as Mina made her entrance—now for the twentieth time—that Henson was more interested in the waves the stagehands made with the tail than in anything she was doing. The only thing she was asked to do was lift her head up high as she entered. It was physically exhausting, a bit like her nude modeling job, but she endured.

Meanwhile, two singers wearing eighteenth-century clothes were singing Mozart to the empty audience. The blue floodlights over them looked cold, and the director had already explained that there would be fake snow during the play. A woman wore a red and gold dress with a hoop, to widen the hips, and a tall, white wig. Beside her was a man in a gray coat and breeches. Of course, as they sang, the audience would not have their eyes on them. They'd be staring at the red dragon with the feathery burlesque hat.

"Keep your head high, Mina," said Henson. "That was fabulous. Absolutely fabulous. You're doing fantastic. Let's try it again, and when you come in from stage right, I want you to walk a little slower but your helpers—guys, for fuck's sake, move the dress up and down, carefully up and then down, with taller strokes, okay? Damn it. How many times do I have to tell you? The audience is watching Mina for the first time. Let her look like waves on the sea coming to the shore. 'Kay? Get those waves high, rolling, rolling up and down and washing onto the sand. We'll have to get this right or we'll spend the rest of the week doing it. Okay? Get it? 'Kay? And not to the side. No one walk to her side. Stay right behind her, single file, carefully and exactly the same distance apart. They don't want to see you. No one wants to see you. No one cares about you. They want to see Mina. All right? Damn it! You all fuck it up and we might as well call it a night. The whole musical will be shit. Right, Toni? Okay? Fuck! … Mina, we'll perform the singing later, 'kay. You'll be accompanying the others on stage, but we'll practice that later. All right, Mina? You're doing fabulous."

She just nodded. She didn't have a microphone, so she couldn't say anything anyway.

"Get back behind her and then we'll have another go. For the hundredth time. Ready?"

She looked out into the audience as she walked on yet again. It was hard to see as all the lights were shining on her. But she could see the shadow of the director. And Toni. She spotted his beanie and his signature theatrical gestures when talking to Henson.

After about the thirtieth take, Henson said, "Okay. Finally. Brilliant! Now bring in the clowns."

THE TAXI PIROUETTE

Mina learned to loathe Daniella. Of course, she was exuberant over opening night being only a month away, but rehearsal was grueling. Her body suffered under the weight of her ridiculous red dress—which was even more unbearable when she sang. Then her acrophobia was toyed with by her practiced performance on the dreaded pedestal. By the time she worked with Daniella in the evenings, the strain was complete. She was asked to perform contortions, spins, and jumps in ways she hadn't thought possible by Dani the choreographer bitch.

After the end of one particularly grueling evening, being made a complete fool of by Daniella's Russian girlfriend, Sonia—a far better dancer than Mina—she was absolutely exhausted. One consolation was that it was Friday, which meant she could sleep in a little tomorrow.

She lugged her large duffel bag through the glass doors of the theater, wearing a long coat over her leotard. It was so late that she turned around and locked the theater behind her. Then she made her way to the side of the street to call a cab.

She shivered, realizing it was not only really late but cold. Then she hailed a cab.

"Hey, Mina."

She recognized the voice immediately. Gail stood by the curb, wearing a fuchsia coat and blue jeans, smiling widely but seeming uncharacteristically reserved.

"Gail? What are you doing here?"

"You told me about this theater. I thought I'd accompany you home. If that's okay? It's Friday and I was … well, I was hoping to join you." Then she looked down the street for a moment. "I texted you but you never returned my messages."

"I've just been so busy."

A cab stopped by the curb. Mina walked toward it, but she wasn't going anywhere. Gail stubbornly stood, obviously vying for her attention. So the cab left.

"We have a new female model," she blurted out.

"Yeah? How is she?" *Oh, Gail, I need to go.*

"Not as cute as you."

"I like men."

"I know." She quickly nodded, putting her hand up. "I know. I hope that isn't … I mean, well, I hope that's not why we haven't talked. That night at your place—"

"I was very drunk."

"You barely drank anything."

Another cab drove down the street.

"Look, can we talk later?" Mina asked, gesturing to the cab. "I'll give you a call. I promise. I told you, I've just been so busy. And I'm so tired, Gail. I have to go."

"Ms. Kuni misses you too. The new girl, her name is Carla, is always late. And she's asking for breaks like ten times a session. Anyway, the class is ending soon, so it doesn't really matter. But when I look at Ms. Kuni, I can tell behind her spectacles that she doesn't like this model. But … I mean, it looks like you got your shit together here, didn't you? I mean, a big Broadway play. Wow. How incredible. I'm so proud of you, Mina. You used to talk about your dream. Now you're living it."

"Thanks, Gail." Another cab stopped by the curb.

"You know," continued Gail, ignoring the cab, "I've been working on painting scenery. You should see my work. You know how I like to ski and stuff back in Colorado. So I've been working on mountain ranges and snow on landscapes. Being that so much of our work in class lately had consisted of flowerpots, I thought I'd expand a little, you know. I've gotten really good—love to show you at my place sometime. I really would like to show you. Perhaps we can arrange a time when you can come over and look at my stuff. Are you still painting?"

Gail's gaze wandered anxiously around the street as she fidgeted with some gold bracelets on her wrist. Then she chewed at her lip.

Mina pulled out her cell phone from her purse to check the time. It was almost ten thirty.

Another cab left.

That's when Gail sort of fell apart. She put her head in her hand and started crying. "Oh, Mina. I miss you. When can we see each other again? I'm your friend. I don't want what happened to come between us. I hope that isn't why things haven't been the same. I just want things to go back to the way they were. I really miss you. I can't believe that—"

"It's not going to go back to the way it was. Not because of you. I only have a month left to get ready for this play. On Broadway. I don't know … honestly, I don't know what the fuck I'm doing." Mina shook her head as Gail wiped her teary eyes with her sleeve. Her sobbing didn't make Mina feel sorry for her; it made her angrier. "Look, it's not just that night. Things have changed. I just need time right now. Maybe we can meet, but just not right now. Okay, Gail?"

Gail nodded solemnly. But she became so serious and that bothered Mina more.

"I mean, we were drunk, I suppose," Gail said with a shrug. "You did what you wanted to do. You touched me first. I was thinking maybe … I don't know, I mean—"

"I don't want to talk about it," Mina snapped. She hailed

another cab. "Anyway, you're not convincing me. Sounds like you're accusing me."

Another cab came by the curb.

"You could have said no, but you didn't. But I'm not accusing you."

"Sounds like you are."

"I'm not. I'm not, Mina. I just want to talk to you. I just want you to answer your phone."

"I don't want to talk about this anymore."

"Well, I want to." And she touched her arm, trying to turn her from the cab. "I mean, not about that. I don't care about that. I just want to talk to *you*. I don't get why ..."

Then silence. No one said a thing. The taxi driver did. He shouted something about having to leave through an open window.

"I have to go, okay, Gail?"

Gail nodded, somber as hell, opening the cab door for her. "Bye, Mina."

"Bye, Gail. I'll call you."

Mina cried the whole way home. She would never see Gail again. For every time she thought about Gail, she didn't think of sex or that Gail was gay. She didn't care about that. She thought about Ms. Kuni and her life before Broadway. Her job, which she had convinced herself, for two years, was a legitimate art job. Modeling wasn't what she had gone to the academy for. She didn't need that sort of work anymore. She was a fucking star. She didn't want to ever go back to that life again. She had been so miserable, barely making enough money to eat. Seeing Gail again would bring that life right back to her.

She whimpered, pressing herself closer to the window so the cab driver wouldn't hear.

Gail knew. Somehow, Gail knew they would never see each other again.

Mina cried for Gail. She felt so guilty because she didn't want to hurt her. But she would never see her again. Never.

And the tears kept flowing.

Or was she crying because she was just tired? Daniella was such a bitch. As much as Mina loved singing for Henson, she detested dancing for Dani. She didn't need to be reminded every day how bad a dancer she was. She knew it. She knew she was only in Toni's play because of her voice. Well, Daniella knew it too but, for some reason, she made it her business to remind her every night.

Gail was her friend.

Maybe she was crying because she was afraid of being alone. After all, who else did she have?

You have me, Christine.

FROM THE FIFTH BALCONY

A BODY HUNG OVER THE RAFTER OF THE TOP BALCONY IN THE theater. It hadn't been taken down yet when Mina arrived. Hanging there motionless under a bright-yellow floodlight, it seemed more like a sick prop or decoration than a person. Mina had been in her changing room when she had heard the screams. She had rushed to the back entrance, through the dark tunnel beneath the theater, hearing shrieks and the sound of her sandals clapping against the stone floor echoing through the tunnel. But she didn't know exactly what all the hubbub was about until she reached the auditorium. Then, as if that were not grisly enough, when she got to the side aisle, stage lights were shining up on the dead body. But the absolute worst was when she recognized the jacket on the body. It was purplish-red and flashy. Gail's jacket. Then she recognized Gail's face.

Mina didn't scream. There was enough of that surrounding her. Nor did she turn away. She just stared, not saying a word. She just stared.

"Oh my God!" Toni was beside her. "Poor girl. Poor, poor girl!" With wide eyes, he turned to Mina. Then it all seemed to register with him, and his surprise turned into a pained look of pity. "Oh Mina, I'm so sorry."

It wasn't until she saw Toni's dreadfully morose expression that it finally sank in that something had happened to her best friend. Gail was dead.

Mina turned from him and closed her eyes. She felt him hold her. Her heart raced and her head spun. She forced herself to turn and look upon Gail's face again. That's when she noticed the oddest thing. Gail's eyes were closed but her youthful face looked serene, oddly tranquil.

"Let's just get out of here," said a girl wearing black tights and carrying a duffel bag.

"I don't think we're going to have rehearsal today," said another.

Henson ran down from the stage, shouting, as if hearing them, "No one leaves! The police are on their way. They'll be questioning us. Everyone stay put. But we're locking all the doors. No one else will be coming in." Then he turned toward the stage. "My God! Turn the fucking lights off! Jesus, as if it isn't horrible enough!"

And everyone obeyed their director, like they always had.

"Oh, Mina … I'm so sorry," Toni said again, gently holding her.

"I don't even understand how she's here," he remarked, more to himself than her.

Then there was weeping. It wasn't Mina. Instead of emitting shouts and cries of shock, people cried and many put their arms around each other. But they didn't know Gail. Only Toni and Mina did. And Toni didn't really know Gail either. If anyone should be crying, it should be Mina. But she didn't cry.

"Mr. Jenny?" a shy young girl in a black leotard asked. She walked up to Henson, who now had his hands on his hips, staring up at Mina's hanging friend. "We ran up to the balcony and found this. There was a note."

Henson looked at the girl strangely, squinting. Then he said quickly, "Hand it to me."

Henson read it and he only seemed angrier. He pushed it to Toni. Then Toni glanced over it, shook his head, and handed it to Mina.

My dear ARTISTS,

Surely this first feat of brilliance is a warning, no? You will henceforth halt all practice of your production. I am sorry it has come to this, truly I am, but it seems that the only way to end further harm to my dear harlequin is a petty show of force. I warn you that if you dare hurt her again, I will deal another. Then there shall be more interruptions. You want to see the horror that lies behind the mask? Look no further. Take a glimpse at the girl hanging from the top balcony who hurt my Christine. The next one will suffer far worse.

Fakers. This is act one of your opening night. Behold what happens when lovers defile an angel. I cannot wait for the final act when my angel falls. Do not touch her. Only on opening night shall we have our end. A fall to end all falls, no?

No loss for words,

Your phantom.

"*Artists,* Mina?" Toni asked, whirling back at her. He stared at her in shock. "*Feat of brilliance?* Those are my words."

"Are you kidding me!" Mina yanked him off her. "What are you saying, Toni? I had nothing to do with this." Then tears finally streamed down her cheeks. She turned from him. "My God, Toni, she was my best friend."

"Si ... si. My God, forget I said it." He laid a hand on her shoulder. "But, Mina ... the words in that note mock me. Those are the words I used to describe the play to you. Who else would use them like this, unless—"

"Unless what? They're your words." She pulled away from him again. "You tell me."

"No," Toni said, shaking his head. "No, they're ours. My God, Mina, I didn't write that. You didn't either. But … if she was your good friend and I didn't, who did? She didn't know me."

Indeed, who?

Henson kept looking up, with his hands in his pockets, probably asking himself the same thing. So did everyone else in the auditorium.

But there was another possible culprit. Not *your* phantom, as he had written. *Her* phantom.

Mina fell into an auditorium seat. She just stared at the stage in shock. She didn't dare turn and look up at the balcony again. Henson leaned over to comfort her, touching her shoulder as Toni had.

"She knew this girl?" Henson asked Toni.

"Yeah. I met her a couple of weeks ago at her apartment."

"Then you two are going to have a lot of explaining to do to the police. But … don't knock yourselves out. Toni, you're the last one who would sabotage this play. And I don't think Mina could hurt a fly."

Mina just stared at the stage. A few others came over to her. She barely noticed them. She felt numb. But numbness was good. Better than crying. She didn't want to do that anymore. She didn't want to feel anything.

What about the voices in my head? My God, maybe it was me?

"Get Mina out of here," said Daniella. She sounded uncharacteristically gentle.

"I'll take her to her dressing room," said Toni.

"No!" Mina snapped. "Not there! Anywhere but there!"

ALONE

M INA DIDN'T ANSWER THE CELL PHONE VIBRATING IN HER COAT pocket. She sat shivering instead. Water trickled down the outside of a metal pipe, forming a very unnatural, yet oddly tranquil, waterfall. It was beside a bench. Mina liked the sound of the water dripping. She turned and looked at the fluffy white frost that covered the pipe. This early in the morning, the water had iced. Strange. Winter had come so fast. She reclined a little more and turned toward the fields, folding her arms. The grass was sprinkled white from frost too. As the sun had just risen, the park was pretty vacant. She was alone. This she usually loved, but not this morning. She really hadn't liked anything all week.

The phantom had gotten his wish. The show had been placed on hold, pending investigation of Gail's suicide. So Mina did nothing, feeling stuck at home like a bird in a cage. But she probably wouldn't have done anything anyway.

For a moment, Mina felt tranquility, enjoying the stillness of the air. She heard a blue jay. A squirrel rummaged through some leaves close to her bench. And for a second, a brief flash, she forgot why she was upset.

Then, between shakes and twitches, she thought of what

had happened. Her closest friend had hanged herself after their fight. Her guilt was nearly as strong as her sorrow. She hated herself. She kept thinking she could have stopped pushing Gail away, especially that night. Maybe Gail came to her because she needed her? Not for their friendship, but over something else? Mina had been so self-absorbed that she only thought of herself. But it was too late. She died.

Monday, rehearsal would start again. What an odd mix of triumph and failure in her life. And yet, Mina Daaé was a star. In less than a month now, she would have her opening show. The biggest show on Broadway.

Mina sighed, leaned on her knees, forced herself up, and walked. She dug in her purse and put on shades. As cold as it was, the sun was out. Then she headed to her favorite part of Central Park: the Mall.

She walked the broad street alone. A couple of stray bicyclists and pedestrians passed, wrapped up in coats, but the park was largely deserted. And so, as she sauntered, her imagination wandered. She wished it hadn't.

She pictured herself wearing that ridiculous red dress with the trailing tail for her first act. She had held her head high, with her tail carried by a hundred clowns somersaulting along the walkway behind her. Mina Daaé, the star of Broadway, the clown. And everyone she passed bowed before their clown. She walked as if it were a parade.

A parade for what? A clown?

Did she murder Gail? Or was it her ghost? Was there any difference?

Ghosts aren't real.

When she was questioned by the authorities, she recounted every step with them. She admitted having spoken to Gail on her way home, but she said she left her on the sidewalk and jumped into a cab. It must have been someone else. It must have been.

But she had locked the doors behind her. She had the keys after being there so late. How did Gail get in? Daniella?

Daniella had extra keys. Could it have been Dani? No. Impossible. That woman was a bitch but hardly a murderer. Sonia? Maybe. But Dani's girlfriend didn't seem to have had much of a motive either.

She looked back at the fields of white and found the place where, not so long ago, she had been sitting. It still had the mark of her body where she had cleared the ice to make space. She shivered some more. It was so oddly frigid for the first weeks of fall.

She admitted she had been angry with Gail. That much was true. That's why she hadn't answered her calls. But Gail hadn't really done anything. When she had touched her that morning, Mina had let her. It wasn't just because of alcohol. Hell, she'd had only two drinks. It was consensual. Honestly, Mina found Gail attractive. But Mina wasn't gay. She felt manipulated. Obviously, Gail had been attracted to her when she started class. That's why she had lunch with her every day. She had probably planned that night months beforehand. That was probably the only reason for their friendship. Just to touch her and make love to her. Right? It was all about sex. Wasn't it? Did it matter? Gail was so nice. Was it that wrong that Gail was attracted to her? Gail was her best friend.

Gail died. She hanged herself by the fifth balcony.

Oh my God.

Mina didn't do it; her phantom did. Her imagined ghost killed Gail. *Imagined?* No, it must have been him. The note sounded like the phantom. The phantom that had infamously tormented her great-ancestor Christine somehow now haunted her.

The theater ensemble all thought it was suicide, but the police officer who had questioned Mina seemed to think differently. The officer acted like it was murder. And based on the notes and the fact that Toni had left the auditorium by three, the investigator seemed sure Mina had killed her. Who else could have done it?

There was no proof. They had let her go.

Her phone buzzed again. Mina sighed and walked off the path. Standing beside a statue, under a tree, she dug through her small purse for her phone. "Huh, what?"

"Hi," Toni said. "Are you feeling all right, Mina?"

"For sure."

"Hmm. You don't sound like it."

Silence.

"Are you coming to my place Friday?"

"Friday? Something happening at your place, Toni?"

"The get-together. Don't you remember?"

Yeah, she remembered. But she couldn't believe they were still having it after the hanging.

"I … I don't think—"

"Mina, I think it would do you some good. You can accompany me. I so want you there. So does everybody."

"It's at your new place?"

"Of course it is. Everyone will be there. I'd love to show it to you. We all want you to come."

"I want to. I really do. It's just … I'm so upset, Toni."

"I am too."

More silence.

Mina walked back to the center of the Central Park Mall. She passed a man on a bike and a woman in sweats "wogging." And then another woman with long blonde hair talking on a mobile phone.

"You still there?" he asked.

"I can't stop thinking how sweet she was. I can't even believe it happened. Gail was such a good friend. And I think she looked up to me, you know. Like a big sister. I … I just feel like I let her down. She was reaching out to me, and I abandoned her. There was so much shit she was going through, and I wasn't there for her anymore. I've just been so busy. I feel so bad. God, if I had known she was thinking of this, I would have done something that night, anything—"

"We've been through this. You didn't do anything wrong. She did it to herself."

"Yeah. After *our fight*. I could have been there for her. And … what about the note? I told you I've been hearing things. I can't …" She took a deep breath and heard her voice cracking. "Jesus, Toni, I can't stop thinking it was me. God. You even said I've been acting weird. God, I—"

"Stop it, Mina. You must stop thinking like this."

"I guess. I can remember everything I did that night. I wasn't with her. I mean, I left her after I got in the cab to go home."

Mina watched a couple walking down the wide walkway, hand in hand. Both wore long coats. The view was romantic, with benches and huge towering trees behind them.

Mina sighed and plopped on the nearest bench beside the walkway.

"She was upset," Toni said. "It was suicide. It's not your fault."

"She never talked about taking her life. Yeah, she was mad at me, but there was never any sense that she was going to kill herself. If I had known that—"

There was silence again. It was almost as if Toni had interrupted her, but he hadn't. He didn't need to. There was nothing he could say to make the situation any better.

She made her way back to the walkway and went all the way to the fountain without hearing Toni, but she knew he was there on the line. She could hear his breathing. And she liked that. By the fountain, she sat down and just stared at the lake.

"Mina, it would mean a lot to me if you came tonight. We're gonna take it easy with rehearsals. I don't think it'll matter much if you have a little fun. And from the little I saw of your friend, and what you told me about her, she wasn't someone who'd mind if you had fun."

"No," Mina said with a chuckle. "Gail never minded fun."

"Mina, I know this is so hard for you. I'm sorry. Really. But, believe it or not, it's been very hard on me. I need to pick up the morale of the crew. And we need you. I need you.

Everyone wants to see you. And I want to see my friend Mina again. Can she come?"

"What should I wear?"

"A semiformal dress. It's a little fancy. But I'm supplying masks by the door."

More silence. "All right."

He took a deep breath. "That is so good. I can't wait to see you." Toni sounded a little like his old bubbly self. "I love you."

"Bye."

THE MASQUERADE BALL

The cab took Mina close to Central Park in northern Midtown. She tapped her long red fingernails nervously on her leg, staring out the window. Her lovely gold-beaded yellow dress draped close to her figure, leaving her back bare. She was adorned with a matching fake gold necklace and saffron high heels—the closest color to her dress—and her hair was up in an elaborate chignon. She looked good, but worried that she had dressed too formally. She had opted for opulence, knowing her good friend Toni.

After going up the elevator to the eightieth floor and being ushered through the door of Toni's penthouse, she was satisfied with her decision. Men with their hair perfectly groomed were wearing double-breasted suits and women wore elegant, long, flowing dresses, some far more expensive than her own. Some, she suspected, wore very real gold and diamond necklaces, too.

Toni's penthouse was breathtaking. The entryway opened into a grand room spanning what must have been nearly half the skyscraper. Everything was modern, with beige painted walls, sharp angles, and walls of windows admiring the Manhattan view. She had to remind herself that the place was

Toni's, her friend's. She remembered him being very poor in France. His benefactors for the upcoming Broadway performance must have paid him plenty for him to have afforded this prized place in Manhattan.

Yet she was reminded that it was Toni when, in the midst of all the formality, Lady Gaga's music blared, with colored lights shining over two small stages, featuring a pair, a man and a woman, in lavender and turquoise tights, dancing sensually. The dancers could have been from his play. She was unsure because, like everyone else in the penthouse, they wore masks.

And that's when a girl handed Mina a mask.

"Ms. Mina Daaé," the girl announced loudly by the entrance.

Nearly a hundred people, who had been socializing, eating hors d'oeuvres, and drinking wine or champagne, cocked their heads, raised their glasses, and hollered out her name. She felt her face redden.

"Hi, Mina," said the girl, with a smile under her purple lace mask. She handed Mina a black lace one. "Cindy," she said quietly with a chuckle.

Mina recognized her. This was Cynthia, one of the other ballet dancers.

"Hi, Cindy."

Cindy chuckled again and touched her arm. "No one knows who anyone is. Isn't that fun? Leave it to Toni. But everybody goes crazy when someone comes in and gets announced. Especially you. Fun, right?"

"For sure."

"It's really good to see you." Cindy leaned forward and kissed her cheek. Then she frowned. "We've all been sad, especially for you."

"Thank you."

"Well," Cindy said, smiling again, "just walk down the steps. You can hang out and dance down in the living room or just wander anywhere. Toni said he doesn't give a shit where we go. He said it's our house. And I know he's gonna be so happy to see you."

Mina made her way through the colorful flashing lights. She didn't recognize anybody, but they kept greeting her. She recognized some of their voices. The living room was full of their bodies swaying to the music.

She wandered into the kitchen. It was even busier there. No one was cooking, but a few people wearing black suits grabbed silver trays and pardoned themselves as they grabbed more food for the guests. So Mina sauntered back through the living room. Less people greeted her as she began blending in with everyone else. Then Cindy called out, "Vince Aster and family" from the front door, and she heard more shouting.

She headed into an adjoining den. Just as in the living room, there were glass tables, curved suede seats, and low couches. It was the same furniture, but the couches were all sorts of ridiculous colors—mauve, pink, violet. And the walls here weren't full of windows; they were covered with paintings.

She enjoyed perusing the artwork. Then her mouth fell open when she saw one of the oil paintings. A rush of fear rose to her chest. This painting was of a king wearing a white puffy outfit, like a clown, with a crown on his head, atop a throne over a desert valley. Blood was oozing along the folds and crevices of his obese body. And blood was being splashed on his face. This was her work. In normal circumstances, Mina would have been super honored that Toni had decided to display one of her works. But that's not what made her dizzy. She clenched her fists and shook her head, trying to calm herself. This was her hallucination. This was the vision she had seen when she had been "drunk" with Gail. Why hadn't she put the two images together? She had vaguely recalled painting it years ago, in Paris, but it had been so long ago and she had never associated it with her dream. Of course, in her dream, the clown had been Toni.

Gail had comforted her after that hallucination. Gail who then …

Get it together, Mina. It's just an old painting.

She shook her head, told herself to stop being stupid, and quickly turned and walked back to the living room.

After greeting Daniella and Sonia, who wore lovely long black dresses and were cordial enough—and were easy to identify because, apparently, they were the only ones refusing to wear masks—and being offered hors d'oeuvres and champagne twice, she headed back into the to-die-for main living room.

The view through the walls of windows was so amazing that it calmed her. She took a deep breath, touched the glass, and looked out at the twinkling lights. But she didn't like looking down.

She spotted her beloved park. The yellow-green lights crossing into the rectangle below her were gorgeous. She couldn't imagine affording a place like this. It must have been, like, a hundred million dollars or something.

"Do you like the view?" asked a man quietly behind her. She would have recognized that Italian accent anywhere.

Mina spun around and put her arms around Toni.

He wore a gray satin mask with a matching gray suit. But his beard hinted at his identity. "I'm so glad you came," he whispered in her ear and kissed her gently on the cheek. "I've missed you terribly."

"How did you know it was me?"

"How could I ever not recognize such beauty?"

Mina cocked her head and squinted. She didn't believe him.

"Cindy told me," he confessed.

"Uh-huh. Well, your place is absolutely breathtaking."

"'Tis." He let go of her and looked out the window beside her. "Well, of course, it's a fortune," he said with a smile. They laughed. Then he playfully wagged a finger at her. "You better not disappoint on opening night or I'll have to sell it."

"I'm already under enough pressure as is." She bit her lip.

"I only jest. But why … you're empty-handed." He raised his glass of champagne. "Would you like a drink?"

"Are we celebrating again?"

"Yes. To the future. No doubt the horrible event has rocked the show, but we will persevere. I must say, I wish I could leave and let someone else run everything now. The stress is—"

"Perhaps you should." Mina gestured to the room. "If you can afford all this, maybe you should go to Santorini and let Vince run things."

"I would never let anyone spoil my circus, Mina."

He tapped on the shoulder of a black-suited server. He grabbed a glass of champagne and handed it to Mina. She hadn't drunk anything since that weird night—that night she had seen him in the desert valley like the man in her painting. But, with his smile, she couldn't refuse.

"I saw my painting in the other room," Mina said, sipping her drink. "I noticed it was not far from a Picasso. Picasso, right? Don't tell me the Picasso is an original? Tell me it isn't. And near my work? Toni? Come on. That's quite a ridiculous compliment."

"Yes, it is a Picasso. And yes, it is his original, near Dalí. But no, it isn't ridiculous next to yours. All these paintings are original, so I hung them up. All three are ar-*tists*."

Mina laughed. "You're mad, Toni. Absolutely mad."

"Si." And he raised a glass with a wink.

Then both of them turned and enjoyed the view again. The music changed to "Mary Jane Holland."

"Lady Gaga, Toni?"

"Are you a fan? I figured the crew had enough of Mozart. I suppose I could have played *The Marriage of Figaro*. Or perhaps Copland's *Rodeo*? Whatever the case, we needed something uplifting. I thought this would be fun."

"Yeah, I'm a fan of Lady Gaga."

"Hmm," Toni said with a solemn nod, raising his champagne glass again. "Me too."

Mina chuckled again and said, "Why the masks?"

Toni cocked his head and folded his arms. "I didn't want to be accosted everywhere I went. I didn't want to run the party like I run my show. I wanted to relax. And, sorry, but I didn't particularly want to have to talk to anyone … except you. See…" He put his hand on her shoulder. "Most importantly, Mina, I wanted to spend time with *you*."

Mina blushed. Then he took her hand and played with her fingers. She turned and watched the dancers, on their mini-raised stages, dancing to Lady Gaga. She didn't pull away from his hand.

She laughed.

"What's so funny?" Toni asked. "With everything that's happened, you don't know what it means to me to hear you laugh."

"Toni, it's just … look around. You're absolutely crazy."

"Thank you," he said with a thin smile and a nod.

Then she felt him pressing along the bones of her fingers.

"No, thank *you*, Toni. You're so sweet."

He gently kissed her on the cheek. "Would my star care to dance with me?"

"To this?"

"No, no." Then he gave a playful smile, let go of her hand, and reached into his pants pocket, taking out a remote control.

"I'm beginning to think you had other intentions than just a party this evening, sir."

Toni shrugged and pressed a button. The song wasn't finished and everyone looked around in surprise. Even the dancers on the stages froze. Then Toni pressed a few more buttons and slow music erupted.

Mina recognized it, of course. Rachmaninoff—probably "Piano Concerto Number 2." Yes, that's what it was. A solitary piano played a lovely soft concerto.

"Would you care to dance with me, Ms. Mina Daaé?" Toni reached for her drink. He put both their drinks down on the floor and held her hand again. "There's enough open space in my living room."

Mina shook her head at Toni's bravado. Any other music would have felt contrived and cheesy. But not this one. Mina loved Rachmaninoff. And Toni knew it.

She nodded.

"You make me so very happy."

They walked hand in hand and many turned, noticing the couple. Toni might have been trying to be inconspicuous, but Mina was quite sure, with his beard and his mannerisms, they all knew their producer. He took her to the center of the room, with her hand raised, and many people moved aside, giving them space. Mina reflected that even now, at this very moment, her friend was producing a show. The change in music and the two of them making their way through surprised guests was drawing everyone's attention.

They took center "stage." A few people yelled out "Toni," but she didn't hear anyone mention her name. Perhaps they didn't recognize her.

They did a simple slow dance, on the wood floor, in the middle of his living room. In this area, all the furniture had been cleared for the party. Before, people had been just bobbing their heads or jumping up and down to hip-hop. Now, a few other couples joined them in the slow dance. The rest stood crowded around the room, watching.

"Perhaps you should have included this one in your play," Mina whispered into Toni's ear as they swayed.

"No, no. That would have been theft of a much higher realm, Mina."

"Why?" Mina asked with a chuckle.

"You see," he said, rubbing her back and bringing her closer, "that would have been like recording your voice. Your voice is angelic, touching God. I would have had no right to steal such a bright light."

"I do believe you're flirting with me, Toni."

"I've been very worried about you," he said, sounding serious. "And I've missed you. I've missed you so. Perhaps being away has shown me that."

All eyes in the penthouse were on them as they swayed. But soon, she lost sight of them. She felt only Toni's embrace. His hand on her waist, his body touching hers, and his beard lightly brushing along her cheek. His cologne. And his trained steps. Even this, the simplest slow dance, he danced professionally. And she let him lead her.

She thought of what he had once said to her over dinner. *Dance is like sex.* She felt close to him like that now, moving in step with him, enjoying the sound of his breath and the touch of his fingers on her back. His hands roamed close to her hips. She felt a desire to be closer, not unlike the frenzied desire she had felt in her apartment, but tempered now. Patient. Love? His embrace made her feel better than she had felt in a long time. But they were just friends. She didn't want to lose their friendship like she had with Gail. And then the thought of Gail made her a little nervous.

"Mina, I love you," he whispered in her ear.

And that was far worse. But no one else could have heard him.

"I'm sorry," he quickly said. "I … I love being with you. Close like this. I really do. I really do like you, Mina. I like you a lot."

"Oh, Toni. I know. I like you too." Mina swayed, patting his back. "I like you so much. I'm so grateful for what you've done for me."

She noticed many others dancing around them now. Married couples or dates, it didn't matter; so many couples were slow dancing close to one another. Some were close enough to caress each other, and others were looking deeply into each other's eyes. It was beautiful.

That's when Toni moved back. Someone was tapping on his shoulder.

"Sir, would you mind if I have a dance with this angel?"

It was said so formally, in an old-school manner. And how could a classy man like Toni refuse? But Mina recoiled when she recognized the stranger's French accent and black mask— a tall, strong man in a flashy red suit and a ridiculous red tail. At first glance, the long, shiny, black mask reminded her of her phantom. But that was silly. After all, the man in her head was a figment of her imagination.

Toni nodded and smiled at Mina. "Till the next time," Toni said.

Then the stranger embraced Mina. And he danced as elegantly as Toni, perhaps better, moving professionally with polished grace. He held her close, too. But when he spoke, she recognized his voice again. And that made her shake.

"Lovely Ms. Daaé, I've missed you. I thought the shock would necessitate a break from my appearances, but it's been hard. Dancing with Antonio—well, that was a bit too much."

She didn't stop. She kept in step with him. She just pulled her head back a little to look at him. She stared at his black mask. This one covered nearly his entire face, but it was similar to what he had worn before, though more elegant, decorated with wavy rows of small glistening diamonds. And he had the same glowing green eyes. This was the fiend. This was the monster who had killed Gail. It had to be, but Mina would have had to be insane to accuse him publicly. He was a hallucination, after all. A figment of her imagination who now danced in step with her.

Her thoughts of Gail, her anger, gave her courage to dance on. Without stopping, she said, "My phantom? How did you get in here, Erik?"

"A night with Princess Charming does me wonders, no? It is quite a psychic effort, I can tell you. But seeing you close to my fuck-clown in this gaudy new penthouse provided me just enough impetus to appear before you as Cinderello. For one night, to dance with my Don Juanita. It is a great pleasure to dance with you, Christine."

"Did you kill Gail?"

"So forward." And he actually laughed. "I thought you did? I like how direct you are. Actually, I pity you. I figured from the note that you must think it was you. That maybe you thought you were losing your mind, perhaps? But surely, now that the phantom who wrote it dances with you, you can be reassured that you are not mad. I am here, in the flesh, dancing with Ms. Christine Daaé."

"You do scare me, Erik."

"Don't be frightened," he said almost mockingly. He turned and swayed with her beside another dancer. It was Cindy, smiling at her while dancing with another man. "Gail wasn't killed by me either. Of course it was suicide. She was in love with you, and you rejected her. I watched the two of you fight, by the street, from a window upstairs in the theater that night. I watched her, in a fit of sorrow, head back into the auditorium, tie a belt around her neck on our prized balcony and hang herself. But don't be upset. I mean, you didn't love her. Did you? You're not gay … are you?"

"You do frighten me. What are your intentions? If you love me, why do you torment me?"

"I am a hideous monster behind my mask, just like you and your fuck-clown. Only your masks are more elaborate."

"Why do you call him that?"

"What?"

"A fuck-clown."

"Because he fucks clowns." And he shrugged as if it was a nonsensical question. Then he led her past two other dancers, closer to the window.

"Toni is the nicest man I've ever known."

"Yes. I suppose he's a good faker, like you."

"How do you know him?"

"I was you in Paris." He smiled and backed up enough to show her those beautiful green eyes, which seemed to hypnotize her. She nearly forgot her hatred for a moment. "I was the Harlequin. Ask him."

"I can't believe you are even here."

"I am, Christine. And … do … do you know why?"

Mina didn't answer.

He stopped dancing and stood still, looking deeply into her eyes. His gaze and countenance seemed so serious. "I want to fuck you, Mina. Really badly, actually."

Gail's words. Those were Gail's words. And it even sounded like her voice. That was finally enough for her to break from him.

Was he making fun of her? The cruelty tore her heart. And incensed her.

In a fit of rage, she slapped him as hard as she could across the face, knocking off his black mask. With horror, Mina finally looked upon Erik. She had expected a scar or disfigurement, but it was more than that. Without the mask, his entire face was full of gashes. Not just the single scar on his right side, which his mask covered, but now it seemed his entire face was disfigured and scarred. His lip was deformed, revealing mottled and broken teeth. His nose was missing and his face was swollen. It was so hideous that she turned away and her rage became disgust.

"Do you see what your fuck-clown did to me, Christine!"

THE BEDROOM

Mina woke in a large bed, facing a wall of windows looking over the twinkling lights of Manhattan. She was lying on top of the covers on the soft bed, still wearing her gold dress. It was oddly quiet. The bedroom was large, with a furry white carpet, modern mahogany furniture, a huge flat-screen TV, and a lovely vanity mirror. It looked like she was still in Toni's suite.

"She's awake," someone said quietly outside the door. "I heard her stir, sir."

When the door to her right creaked open, she feared it would be her ghost. But it wasn't. It was Toni. His mask was off and he was looking down at her with such concern. He had taken off his suit and was wearing just a simple T-shirt and sweats. He sat by the edge of the bed and ran his hand over her shoulder.

"Mina, I think you weren't ready for this."

"Did you see him? Did you see that man? The man who killed Gail?"

"Che?" Toni squinted and quickly shook his head.

"The man I danced with after you."

He shook his head again. "Vince wanted to introduce me

to a new actress. There was no one else who danced with you after me. You were alone."

"No. It was Erik. I danced with him. The man I danced with was Erik."

His expression of confusion changed to fear. He quickly turned from her.

"What's the matter, Toni? You did see him?"

He shook his head. He laughed nervously. "You're giving me a fright, Mina, saying that name. I wish you wouldn't say that name."

"Erik?"

He nodded and turned back, forcing a smile. "Erik was someone I worked with many years ago."

"Yes!" Mina sat up in bed. "Yes. So you saw him?"

He shook his head. Then he quickly, but gently, took her hand and laid her back down on the bed. He smiled. "Calm down, dear. You have to just rest."

But her heart was racing and she was having trouble breathing. She shook her head. "He came to me tonight. Butted in on our dance. He denied having killed Gail. He said Gail committed suicide."

"Gail did kill herself."

She nodded. "He said he had nothing to do with it. But he started spewing all kinds of things about you. He said he hated you. He called you a fuck-clown. Erik said you—" She stopped.

Toni looked pale and his face looked pained.

"What? What's wrong? I keep seeing him, Toni. God, I'm afraid! I see him in my sleep. I see him, God, I see him every-where. I hear him in the cab. I hear his voice in the morning. He laughs at me. Taunts me. I hear him in the dark. I see him reflected in the window when the cab takes me to the theater. I must be going crazy … I don't know. I think I … I think I did kill Gail. God! Not because I wanted to. I loved her. But I think I'm losing it. I saw a vision the night before you met Gail. I saw you covered in blood. It was just like your painting, but the clown was *you*. And Erik invited me in to see you bleed. He hates you."

Mina laughed and that seemed to upset Toni even more. "I see him everywhere. I saw him performing the morning I fell during my audition. He's been coming to me ever since you gave me the part. Do you know him? His name is Erik. Erik."

"Erik Belles?" Toni asked, with eyes a little too wide to be normal. "Si. I know Erik Belles. And I remember the words *fuck-clown* too."

"Yes. Yes. Thank God! Maybe I'm not crazy. That's what he said his name is. Erik."

"Erik used to work for me. Where did you hear that slur: *fuck-clown*?"

"He wrote the note, Toni."

Toni took a deep breath and slowly shook his head. "No, Mina. No. He didn't. That's impossible."

"Yes, he did. He said that he came tonight to make me feel better." Mina laughed. "Can you believe that? He's sadistic. He acted like, after he took my hand from you to dance, he acted like he was doing me a favor by seeing me. To prove that I'm not crazy. To prove that I didn't kill Gail. He said that Gail took her own life."

She turned on her pillow and stared at the yellow wall. The yellow in the shadows in the dim evening light matched her golden dress.

She heard Toni breathing but he had stopped talking. He just sat over her, rubbing her shoulders and back.

Most of the light in the dimly lit room was cast by the city lights outside. She looked back at the large window, facing the incredible view.

"Mina, you danced with yourself. You swayed alone. Vince came up to me to introduce me to one of his friends, and we stopped dancing. Then I looked over and caught you just swaying back and forth to the music. I thought you were just enjoying the music, but I saw you close your eyes and put your arms in the air as if around someone. Now I get it. No one thought anything of it, because we love you. But I thought it was odd. Now I understand you thought you were dancing with someone."

"I was!" Mina snapped, spinning around to look at him.

He had a smile now. He was back to being the kind Toni she loved. He gently shook his head.

"Then you went to the window in the living room," Toni continued. "I heard some gasps and rushed back to you. I picked you up from the ground where you had fallen. Then you fainted again in my arms."

"Is this your room?" she asked, looking around.

"Si."

"And the party?" She sat up, but Toni helped her down again. "Oh, I'll get right back to the party. You need to attend to your guests."

"The party ended three hours ago."

Three hours!

That did it. She felt an out-of-body sensation, as if she were finding out that her life was unreal. Like everything was a dream. Like she was falling forever. She needed Erik to pinch her skin again. But this was reality. *Her* reality. Not a dream, or maybe some kind of nightmare. Mina stared at Toni and shook her head.

Ended three hours ago!

She felt a tear on her cheek. Her hands shook. Her heart pounded.

"I'm scared, Toni. I … I don't know what's happening to me. I keep fainting like a stupid, weak girl. And ending up waking in places … and seeing things. What's wrong with me?"

Toni took her shaking hand and leaned down and hugged her gently. Then his eyes teared up too. "I don't know. But it will be all right. Rest. Forget everything. Don't worry. Forget about all of it. I only care about you. You have me so worried. Whatever's happening to you, I think it's the stress of the play.

Yes, Gail killed herself. God, Mina, you're dealing with enough. Don't feel guilty, as if that were your fault. It wasn't. Don't ever think that again."

"Maybe it was Erik? I don't like him. I don't trust him."

"It couldn't have been Erik, Mina. Erik died years ago."

DINNER AT TONI'S

Toni constantly watched over Mina the whole weekend, insisting that she spend the nights as a guest in his own bedroom. He wouldn't let her leave, checking up on her every few hours and having Jacque, his butler, serve her meals as if she were a queen. When Monday morning came, with the return of rehearsals, they were driven to the theater in his Bentley. Then he sat quietly in front-row center seats the whole day, staring up at the stage while she rehearsed the second act under the witch, Daniella. The attention made her feel silly, but she never spoke to him. Come to think of it, she had barely even spoken to him the whole weekend. But when the afternoon rehearsals came to an end, and Daniella wanted to torture her some more with extra evening dance lessons, Toni intervened and took Mina back to his penthouse.

Dinner was incredible. He might as well have met her in a fancy restaurant. They sat alone every night, like tonight, in a dining room with a wall of glass affording a gorgeous view of the twinkling lights of the New York skyline. Toni sat across from her at the middle of a long oak dining table that looked like an antique. Behind him was the breathtaking vista of Manhattan.

Jacque brought in an ornate dish of roasted duck decorated in garnish, surrounded by feathers, on a silver tray. Jacque was a short man with auburn hair and a mustache, wearing a black suit with a tail. He methodically cut two slices of meat and placed them on silver plates. Then, ridiculously, he cut them into small, edible pieces. He put a serving of fresh, steamy bite-sized potatoes, green beans, carrots, and kale on each plate. Then he drizzled a sauce over their steamy plates. No, the finest restaurant could not have served her better. Red wine was poured in two lovely crystal glasses.

Far in the background, Mina heard music—Mozart, of course. It was so elegant. But the funniest thing about the whole affair was that Toni was wearing a black T-shirt and gray sweats. And Mina had on a simple silk blouse and black slacks. She had even washed off most of her casual makeup after the rehearsal. But Toni had readied himself in his room before dinner, showering, combing his short hair perfectly, and even applying cologne. It might have been casual, but the restaurant ambiance made it feel a little like a date.

"I really should go after this," Mina said.

"No." Toni smiled, biting into the duck, and raised a finger. "No, no. Stay. Stay longer. Please. You've given me such a scare, Mina. Once I know you're better, you can go. Consider this insurance. I must help the star of my show."

"Well, you've helped, Toni." She chuckled. "Thank you. You've helped a lot. And you're right. After yesterday, it would have been hard for me to come in today."

"So," he said with a grin and a broad hand gesture. "What's the problem? Mi casa, su casa, as they say. I'll wait for whatever it takes for you to recover."

"Okay, Toni."

"You did very well today. I feel like the show is going so much better now. There's less of a shadow in the air from what happened. I know the dancers, at least, are back to laughing."

"And I'm singing."

"Si," he said with a warm smile. "I couldn't ask for more than that. Things are starting to settle back in again."

"For sure."

She dipped the duck in the sauce at the edge of her plate. It was exquisite. "I heard Vince is spreading gossip around that I have seizures to explain my falls?"

"Could be true," Toni said with a shrug. "Of course, I don't want anything to be wrong with you, but it would be nice if there was an explanation. Do you want me to go with you to your appointment with the doctor Thursday?"

"Oh stop, Toni. You've done enough already."

"You could have some sort of seizure condition, you know. I'm so worried about you."

She sipped some wine and nodded. The red wine was smooth and delightful. "Wouldn't it be nice if all I needed was medication? I don't know. I'm just worried that if I faint again, it could ruin the show."

"Stop worrying. Everything will be fine." He smiled but his grin was fake.

Toni was more worried about this show than anyone else.

It fell silent. Mina didn't mind. She just heard the sound of their silverware scraping the plates. And lovely Herr Mozart playing in the background.

She gazed in rapture at the view behind him while enjoying every morsel on her silver fork, all the while catching his stray glances at her. Indeed, she was grateful. He cared about her. But she felt uncomfortable when their eyes met in the candlelit room.

"How did you know Erik?" she asked.

That question seemed to be the last thing he'd expected. He lost his smile. Then he wiped his beard and quickly turned to the window. "We shouldn't talk about that. It, it, could bring back what happened."

"I know. But Toni, I feel like if you tell me, I'll be less worried. If he's real, maybe I'm not crazy, you know? Just like seizures. Maybe there's something going on that can help explain things? I mean, it's not just Gail now. I'm freaked out about sleeping for so long through the party. I still don't even know what happened."

He nodded slowly but hesitated. "You don't understand. I wasn't only talking about you. I don't want to bring back what happened between Erik and *me* either."

"Please, Toni. Tell me. How did you know him?"

"He was a good friend," he said with a sigh. "Like you. But it was years ago. You remember my calls? I told you about a man I had met who could both dance and sing. A man who was the shining light of my show."

"Yes. I think I remember. Tell me about him."

He nodded. Then he traced the stem of his wine glass with his finger, staring at it.

After he didn't say anything, Mina said quietly, "Please, Toni."

"In Paris…" He stuffed some meat into his mouth, looking like it was more of a chore than a pleasure. "We had the circus, if you remember. I worked on it while I taught. Loved it. But I didn't focus everything on it until after you left."

"So you said. You stopped teaching."

"Yeah," he said with a nod. "Well, after I met him, I decided to devote everything to the show. Erik was a unique soul. A boy bounding with energy."

Mina dipped more delicious meat into the sauce and tasted it.

He sighed. "We met in a café, of all places. Not the theater. Over cappuccinos, we hit it off. I tell you, he had so much energy, it was infectious.

"But I didn't know at the time he was destitute. No, not just destitute … desperate. He had run from affluence, preferring madness. You know, what we call *art*. He had no money. Everything was about art. But watching him, even that first time in the café, made me realize that, like you, he was a star."

"Really, Toni?" she said with a chuckle, feeling her cheeks blush. "Like me? How? How could you tell? Especially in a café?"

"I just knew."

"And like me?"

"Look at you. Your voice is not the only thing that touches God. Look at your face."

"Please, Toni," she said, turning from him.

"'Tis true. Anyway, I'm quite astute at finding talent. And beauty. Erik and you." He stopped and drank wine pensively. Then he took a deep breath and turned away from her, preferring the view again.

The butler returned, swinging open the door. It was so still that, even though he had just walked through the door, it felt like he was bounding in a rush. "Antonio, are you and Ms. Daaé going to want chocolate soufflé? I need time to prepare."

Toni turned back to Jacque with a faint smile and said, "No. Thank you." But then he squinted at Mina. "Oh, but how 'bout you? Jacque makes an incredible chocolate soufflé. You really should taste it."

"No. I don't think I'll fit in my costume if I do that."

"Just coffee, Jacque," Toni said with a laugh. "With perhaps a pinch of chocolate."

Toni sat sideways, looking outside, sipping more red wine and staring pensively out the window again. It was as if he was done with his story.

"He had acted in various plays," he continued. "But his true talent was dance. He was so graceful, incredible move-ment, so flexible and fluid. I never would have thought someone could move like that. Especially a man. It was so odd that a dancer with so much talent met me in a simple café." He sighed, forked a couple of potatoes, and ate some. Then, with his mouth full: "I got to know him. We became the best of friends. You can figure out the rest. That's all."

It didn't sound like that was all. It sounded like there was hours more.

"He probably met you on purpose at the café," Mina said. "You were known for the theater even when I was your student."

"I thought that. I suppose, after seeing him perform so well at the audition, it sure seemed planned to me too at the time, though."

"Rehearsal or audition?"

"Audition." Toni laughed. "I hadn't seen him perform like I saw you perform in the university, darling. He was good. Incredible. I was shocked at his gracefulness. In tights, he danced elegantly, even better than you."

"Really?"

"Even besting my angel, Mina, si. Well, you can guess where this is going. I hired him for the show."

"I remember you telling me about a dancer after I came to New York. You fell in love with him, if I remember?"

He looked disturbed by that. He ran his hand over his head and shook it quickly, turning stern again. "Mina, I don't want to talk about this."

"No, please. Please go on. I feel like if I know, I'll better understand who this man is and why his ghost is haunting me."

"There's no ghost. Erik never went to the US. He was born in Strasbourg. He could barely speak English. Whatever vision you saw, it wasn't Erik. Could be a phantom, like the legendary phantom that haunted your great-ancestor Christine. But not my Erik. Unless you spoke with him in French."

"I speak to him in English most of the time. He has an accent. I speak to his ghost. And he wears a mask too."

"Oh Mina, come on."

"You saw the note. You know it wasn't you. So either I'm insane or there's a ghost haunting our play. Please go on. Tell me so you can prove I'm not crazy. Is he the man you fell in love with?"

"You're not crazy."

"Then tell me. Was this the man you spoke of that you fell in love with?"

He didn't respond. But that was the answer.

Mina dipped some potato into the sauce. The sauce was salty and sharp. Exquisite. She could have just dipped the fork in the sauce and enjoyed it alone. She ate more and, for the moment, didn't care if Toni stopped telling his story. It was all so delicious.

"He played the Harlequin," Toni finally admitted. "He had your role."

Mina had a little difficulty swallowing. The role that Erik had told her, time and time again, would make her fall.

"And … I suppose he knew me as well as you do. Si, if my Erik was conjured up from the grave, he could have written that note."

"Tell me about him."

"Mina."

"Please."

"I loved him." He flashed a fake smile. "I'm not really gay, but you should have met him. If you knew him, you'd understand. Any man would have been attracted to him."

"I don't have a problem with whether you're gay. I'm not anti-gay."

Of course she wasn't. She had sex with Gail before she died. And, for a second, Toni looked at Mina smugly, as if thinking—*obviously*.

"I'm not gay," he replied. "I don't have a problem with it either. But I'm not gay. I don't even think I'm bisexual. I experimented, I suppose. It's … it's difficult to explain. Erik was more than a man or a woman. He was…" Toni raised his hand, staring at his fingers, trying to gesture something to make Mina understand, but then his hand dropped. He smiled. "He was a god. An Adonis. Like the *David*. You should have seen him. Pretty and handsome. Exuberant. All of it. Our theater was a paltry dump of rats, dust, and filth at the time. And so, when Erik performed his ballet, the audience thought they were going to see a circus. No. No, not Erik. When the light shone over him, my Erik, just Erik in the center of the stage, he held everyone's attention with his perfection. Everything—the seats, the audience, everything in the auditorium—became unimportant. Only Erik's movements mattered. He was more like a light than a human form; he moved as if he wore skates: gliding, jumping, and twirling, as fast and smooth as an ice skater. It was something I had never seen—something I will never see again. They watched him spin and twirl. He was so good. All eyes turned to him, just as all ears turn to you.

"Many of the movements Daniella showed you were choreographed by him. He was our original choreographer. You once asked why I stole from Mozart. I didn't. No. No, I stole from my Erik."

He fell silent again, just nodding to himself.

Mina stared at him in the dim light of the room. She didn't care for the view or the food anymore. She was captivated by him and this story.

He was so serious, almost solemn. It was a side of Toni she didn't see often except, when she thought of it, when he was alone with her.

But most importantly, for the first time in months, someone was talking about her hallucinations. Perhaps she wasn't crazy? Whatever the case, it was quite clear that Toni had loved this man.

"Toni, did you have a falling out with him?" Mina finally asked. "Is that why you never mentioned him again?"

"Fall? No … I loved him."

"Then what happened?"

"A fall," Toni said, chuckling and nodding. "Hmm. Si, si, indeed, that's it, Mina. It was a fall, but not over love. I told you my circus in Paris was in the American style, where classical music did not fit jugglers and acrobats. The introduction with the ballet pieces was different. It was the opposite of our

Broadway play. In Paris, it was a circus invaded by Mozart; in Broadway, it's Mozart invaded by the Big Top. Of course, Erik exhibited high class with his feet. But, well, one night he fell from the tightrope in the third act. Unlike you, he had no net."

"Oh no," Mina cried, putting her hand over her mouth.

"He was instantly paralyzed. He never danced again."

"Oh my God."

"Si. He never walked again." And that was too much. Toni put his head in his hand. Then, in a broken voice, he said, "And he blamed me, Mina."

"I'm so sorry, Toni."

"It's been so long, I thought I had gotten over this. When you fell, it brought the horror right back to me."

"Can you describe him?"

"Che?" he asked, looking up in surprise. "Why? … I did. He was the most beautiful man I had ever known. What more can I say?"

"No, I mean, can you actually describe his features."

Jeesh, can you be any colder, Mina. But I have to know!

"Toni, I saw him during the audition. Or I dreamt him up. Then I danced with him in your house. I even see him in my dreams. Can you tell me what he looked like?"

"Why?"

"Did he have bright-green eyes? And a goatee?"

Toni stared at her and grew pale again. He didn't say a word.

"And scars running from his forehead down his right cheek? A disfigurement along his nose?"

"Stop," Toni cried. He jumped up. "Stop it."

"Toni, I'm sorry, I—"

He stared up at the ceiling and cried, "Mio dio! Mi perseguiti anche adesso?" And he slammed his fists against the window overlooking the view.

"I don't speak Italian, Toni."

Mina jumped when the dining room door swung open.

Jacque walked in, carrying another silver tray. This one had two white porcelain mugs and a silver coffee brewer. He poured fresh coffee into both cups.

"Give her a little chocolate," Toni said dismissively with his back still turned.

Jacque smiled at Mina and nodded.

Toni ran his hand along his beard, staring out the window. "Jacque knows just the right amount to make it exquisite."

"What is it, Toni?" she asked him, as the butler drizzled melted chocolate in her cup. "I … I don't know Italian."

Toni sat back down and ran his hands through his short, feathery hair. "Did you see footage from the old show? That must be it. I thought everything had been taken down from so long ago. I tried to get rid of everything."

"I didn't."

Jacque bowed and quickly left the room.

"Of course he had a scar on his face," he answered, as if she were dumb. "A head injury. Probably much more damage underneath. He was never the same after the fall. I told you, he never walked again. And a joyful man became depressed and bitter. As tragic as Gail, I guess. And green eyes. Yes, the brightest green I had ever seen."

"So, it is him. What happened? How did my phantom die?"

"No," Toni said, shaking his head. "Not your phantom. Stop this! I can't believe you saw him. It's just not true. You must have seen an old picture of the performance."

"Is that any better? Then we're back to me being crazy. That's why I have to know."

"Please, Mina, not tonight. Let's not talk any more of this."

He made his way around the table and crouched down on a knee, leaned over, and gently kissed her cheek. "Goodnight, cara Mina. You can use my bed again. I am so happy for you to stay with me one more night."

"Wait a minute." Mina snatched his arm. "What

happened to him? You're not finished. You said he never danced again. You didn't say how he died. Oh Toni, tell me. How did he die? Please. You have to tell me!"

"Just know that he died. There's nothing else to tell."

And he was going to get up, but she grabbed him again. She shook her head. Then she ran her hand along his short, feathery hair. "I'm staying for you to help me, right?" she asked. "To feel better? So finish your story. I need to know what happened to him. If I can put reality into this, then I'll know that, perhaps, I'm not crazy."

"Mina, please. Forget it."

"You have to!" Mina snapped. She searched his eyes. He actually smiled at her outburst. Oh, she adored Toni. They never fought. Even when he had taught her onstage and she forgot lines, he was always patient, respectful, and kind. But she had to know.

How did Erik die? How was his ghost a threat to her?

He started getting up again. This time she brought him close and pressed her lips hard against his. He gasped in surprise, blowing against her lips. Then she pressed harder, licking and bringing her tongue along his while she pulled his body close. She ran her fingers along his short hair again as she kissed him.

"Tell me," she said between kisses. "Or else."

"Or else, what?" he asked, laughing. "What are you talking about?"

"Or else I'm fucking you in your dining room."

"Mina, you *are* crazy." And he laughed nervously, backing away. "I don't have to tell you anything anymore. You just proved you are crazy."

They laughed again. But she pressed her lips passionately on his again, as if ready to carry out her threat.

"There's not much else to tell," he said, gently pulling from her. He looked down for a moment and lost his smile. "It's terrible."

"Please, Toni."

"I ruined his life. He turned to drinking. He lived off the streets. He sold himself." He turned his head from her and tried to get up, but Mina kept a vise-like grip around his arm. He looked down at it and nodded slowly. "Soon he really didn't have to blame me—I blamed myself. Time passed and I missed him. I loved him. Si. I will always love him. Just as I will always love you. But more, I felt responsible. The stage-hands were paid a paltry wage. The horrible mistake and neglect in safety wasn't all that surprising."

And he met her gaze. Tears were forming in his eyes, and it made her want to weep too.

"I just didn't have the money … One day, on a frigid, snowy day, I saw him near the theater. He was without shelter. I took him in. Cared for him. Let him stay with me, like I am letting you stay with me now. And finally, in the evening, I asked him what I could do to fix this. I told him I'd do anything for him." He laughed bitterly. "He suggested the one thing I didn't want to do. He wanted to perform in my play again. What's more, he wanted to go up to that pedestal. Of course I refused. We fought, as we often did. He called me a *fuck-clown*. Eventually, after being called enough stupid names and being reminded far too many times that he had nothing left to live for because of what I had done to him, I capitulated.

"He thought of singing *Don Giovanni*. He couldn't dance, but he could sing. He may not have had the voice you have, but he had vision. So you see, it was not Herr Mozart that I had robbed; it was Erik. We had used Mozart, snippets from *The Marriage of Figaro*, with our choreography for years, but never *Don Juan*. But Erik *was* Don Juan, for women and men. Literally a living libertine, more so than anyone I had ever known. Even with his disfigurement, his body was attractive. And he had used sex to woo both men and women, even as a paraplegic. Now, asking to be back in my play, he wanted to fight his challenge and conquer it. So he devised a plan to sing up on that ledge. It was a way to thumb his nose at death."

He stopped and lowered his head onto her shoulder.

"Oh, Toni."

"At first, I didn't want to do it. I thought it was a terrible idea. He wanted to go right back up to the pedestal where he had fallen. We'd have to carry him up the ladder for the final act.

"It was this performance, Mina, that got us our fame. We made the fall as real as we could, just like in our Broadway play. The audience filled the stadium and watched the whole show just to see our finale. Whereas before they had watched his body, now they listened to his voice and his performance. Just as they do with you now. The strange accompaniment of Mozart and the Big Top. The singing was scant in the rest of the play, but we gathered up all the money we could for the finale, even adding an orchestra. I felt I owed him. Hell, I told you, I would have done anything to make him better. And it worked, for a little while. The audience loved him. It was such a bizarre twist in the act. I heard his voice and it touched God, like yours. He was so talented, Mina. He was, like you, a star."

He paused. But then … he wept bitterly.

"Oh, Toni, what's the matter?" She embraced him while he was still on his knees, crying.

"That … that is how he died," he said, with a shaking voice, between sobs. "I killed him. That's why I didn't want to say. It was because of me. It was my fault. You asked. That's how he died. He gave up, not only because he couldn't walk, but because he couldn't dance. His dream. The singing was a temporary thing. I destroyed him."

He stopped talking and wept more in Mina's arms. Then, when finally able to speak again, he said, "One night, we had a huge fight. You see, despite success, he told me many times that all he had ever wanted to do was dance. I had destroyed that. He drank too much, as he often did. But the intensity of the fight was different. We carried him to the top of the tightrope pedestal in the final scene, as we always had. Of course, now there was a net below. Only he made sure to cut it on that final night. I should have known. He said it would be the best show ever. He kissed me before we went on and whispered in my ear, 'in boca al lupo,' which in Italian is like saying 'break a leg.' The whole end performance was no longer a ruse. It was real."

Toni stopped talking. He even stopped crying. He just froze in her arms.

"God, Toni, I'm so sorry." She kissed his forehead. "Forgive me for asking. Forgive me."

"No. No. I understand."

She didn't let him go. She held him like a mother holds a baby, cuddling and swaying, back and forth, with him in her arms. She went right back to kissing him, now gently along his beard, neck, and forehead. She held him tight.

"You're too good to me," he said.

"Me? How could you say that, Toni? After everything you've done for me here, how can you say that?"

"I don't know how you saw him. I tried to get rid of all traces of him. Not because I didn't love him, but because of what I did to him. I couldn't face seeing him. I couldn't look at him … It was my fault. *Fuck-clown*, indeed. I didn't want to be reminded … of what happened."

Toni gently pushed Mina away. "The show went on. His show. And you know what? It became more popular after he died. Despite what happened, in honor of him, we didn't change the ending. I know that's what he would have wanted. You know the rest. My friends pulled together all their money and used a different ensemble. *The Harlequin* took off in Europe. I only wish he had been alive to see it."

"I'm so sorry, Toni."

She kissed him gently again. He nodded. She turned his head and their lips met. She ran her hand under his T-shirt and felt his belly and chest. She cradled his head in her arms again.

"I'm sorry I made you tell me."

"Whatever is happening," he said, hugging her close, whispering in her ear, "I do believe his spirit visits you. Whether in your mind or as a ghost, I believe the phantom haunts you. I don't think you're crazy. And I wish he'd stop."

"It must be Erik. Thank you for telling me."

Their kisses became more passionate, and they groped each other harder. Mina ran her hand under his shirt, rubbing his belly again. Her hand wandered over his back and along his hip. Then she touched his pants and rubbed over his cock.

"Oh, Mina." He laughed nervously. "I'm just a foolish old man."

"You've been so kind to me. First the part, then the support when Gail died. Why? Why are you so nice to me? I don't deserve you."

"I don't deserve you." He started to smile but then became very serious.

Their eyes were locked.

Her heart raced. "Why did you do this for me? Why have you been so patient with me, Toni?"

"I care about you."

"No," she whispered. She kissed his lips again. "It's more, isn't it? You're not a shy man. What did you say while we danced? Or did I dream that too?"

"What? I don't remember."

"You remember." She brought his lips to hers, hard, again. Then she ran her hand down toward his pants. She reached under the sweatpants and ran her fingers along the skin of his hard cock. He moaned. "What did you say when we danced? Say it. Say it to me again. Please, Toni. I want to hear that too. Do you remember? What did you say?"

She gently pulled down his sweatpants and held the bulge in his underwear.

"Mina, I'm an old man."

"That's not what you said."

"I said I love you. Ti amo. I love you. But … I haven't

been with anyone since Erik. I can't ask anything from anyone anymore."

She shook her head and unbuttoned her blouse. He stared at her bra. Then she helped pull off his shirt.

"Don't blame yourself, Toni. It's not your fault."

There was no more crying. Just the two of them in the quiet room, making out like school kids for the longest time. But it was funny, because neither could go any further. She didn't care. She wanted to kiss forever. Mina figured that they both still feared damaging their friendship. And yet they couldn't disengage.

Then he surprised her. With her eyes closed, kissing his lips, she felt her body being lifted onto the table. She sat on the wooden table while they resumed kissing. She felt wet between her legs. "I think I'm in love with you, Toni. No … I know I am. I love you too."

"We don't have to do this," he said, backing up and looking seriously into her eyes.

She answered him by reaching back and unclasping her bra, throwing it to the side. His eyes stared hungrily at her naked breasts. Then—in the frenzy, she wasn't sure if he took them off or she did—her slacks were unzipped and pulled down. Then came her lace panties. She was naked, sitting on the table in his elegant dining room. He ran his hands along her nude body as she cocked her head back, looking at the to-die-for view of the city.

"Here?" he asked, dipping down and sucking her nipple. "Now?"

"Sure." Then she smiled. "I saw how you looked at me in rehearsal today. Please take me. I said the dining room, remember?"

"You said if I didn't tell you." He laughed between kisses. "I told you."

Then she felt a hand along the curves of her boobs as another touched between her legs. She moaned.

"You are beautiful. So beautiful, Mina."

"Touch me. Yes. Rub me. Do it. Harder."

He obliged. His other hand ran down to her waist; then she arched up and he ran his hand along her ass. He settled between her legs and rubbed her gently like she had once rubbed him in her apartment. His finger ran along her crotch and then entered her.

"Harder," she whispered in his ear. "Yes, Toni. Inside. Please. Fuck me."

He obliged. She felt his finger wander inside and out while they met each other's lips yet again. Her butt was pressed against the cold wooden table as she arched her back and pressed her breasts against his chest. She felt his finger, then two, deeper inside her, and she moaned. She moaned louder, but he stifled her orgasms with his lips and tongue. He rubbed repeatedly, faster, until her whole body lurched up into his hand with her final orgasm.

She closed her eyes for a moment and took a deep breath. Then she looked at him. His eyes were still bloodshot, but hungry, as they gazed at her tits and along her naked body. "That was so good. Oh, God, Toni, that was good … So good … Now take me inside. Fuck me on your table." She said it almost in a whisper. "Please. Fuck me, now."

She closed her eyes. There was a pause, almost a hesitation, where all she felt was his hand caressing her hips and his warm breath. His hands moved along her legs and touched her breasts. His hard cock brushed against her knee. He grasped her waist, and she sucked his tongue, kissing him in rapture.

He entered her and pushed into her as she flexed her butt against the hard table. She ran her hands along his ass and felt the crack as it flexed. He moved in and out of her. He moaned. Then he caressed her breasts again, running his lips down to her hard nipples and sucking them while continuing to thrust hard inside.

As he moved closer, breathing heavily, she heard the door. She looked over as the door cracked open, but it quickly shut.

The interruption didn't stop Toni. But he was careful, so gentle, even now. He ran a finger delicately along her face, as if tracing her, while he closed his eyes and thrust. Mina imagined he was feeling the curves and texture of her so he could recreate it in a painting or a sculpture later. His finger glided over her thin eyebrows and ran along her lips. She touched the hairs along his chest and wrapped her arms around him, embracing him and bringing him closer. She heard the sound of them together, their wetness, while his fingers traced over her sharp nose. Then his fingers brushed her cheek and slipped inside her mouth. She sucked a finger as he continued to thrust.

Then she closed her eyes and glided her fingers along his face, doing the same to him. She ran her fingers over his bushy beard and his eyebrows, then along the soft, feathery hair of his head, which she loved. She opened her eyes, and he was smiling at her as his whole body pushed into her faster. Harder. She groaned with the pleasure she so desired. That seemed to spur him on more. Again and again, he moved inside her until she grabbed him with the sudden animalistic fervor she'd felt when she'd thrown him against the wall of her apartment months before. She pulled him in as close as she could, lifting herself onto him hard, and that's when she felt him quake and orgasm inside her.

"Oh, Toni."

"I love you," he said. He leaned over her, panting. "I love you, so much."

But as he leaned on his side, he opened his eyes wide all of a sudden, seemingly confused, almost afraid.

"What's the matter, babe?" she asked, running her hand along his thin hair.

"There wasn't any protection," he said, shaking his head.

"I don't care." She leaned her head against his and

smiled. Then she turned and kissed his lips. "Even if we make a baby, I love you, Toni. I know that now. I wouldn't ever regret it. I love you. I love you so much."

"Yes. I love you, Mina."

THE YELLOW WALLPAPER

Mina blinked her eyes, gazing up at a single maple beam running along the center of a vaulted wooden ceiling. She was sunk in the most comfortable mattress she'd ever lain on in her life, digging her head into the softest of pillows. It was quiet. In front of her, through the wall of windows, was an absolutely breathtaking morning view of New York City. She stretched her arms, wearing a soft, white satin camisole. Then she realized she had woken up alone. This was a surprise, for Toni had slept with her every night since their romantic dinner.

The sound of squeaky wheels and the clang of porcelain, or glass, made her turn toward the door to her right. Jacque, wearing what seemed to be the same suit he had worn last night, quietly lifted a silver lid from a plate on a wheeled cart. She stretched and yawned again.

"Oh, mademoiselle, I'm sorry to have woken you."

"Do you know what time it is, Jacque?"

"Around eleven thirty."

"Oh, God, I slept in that long?"

"Don't fret. Mr. Vollini wants you to rest. It's Saturday. He wants you to take the whole day off."

"He's too good to me."

"Me too," Jacque said with a gentle smile.

Then she remembered. Just as he had insisted on her sleeping over, he had insisted she not work this weekend. She imagined the stir this must have caused the crew, particularly her choreographer bitch, Daniella, who had asked for additional practices over the weekend.

"I think I could sleep all day here," she said with a yawn, turning on her side and digging her head back into her pillow.

"Perhaps you should. Don't worry yourself, Miss Daaé. Mr. Vollini said he'd return around five. He only desires that you rest."

And with that, the butler dipped his head, his short hair perfectly groomed, and walked out of the room, closing the door behind him.

Mina eventually removed the covers, crawled out of bed, and enjoyed the feel of the soft, fluffy white carpet under her naked feet. She dug her toes along the floor, its softness and thickness reminding her of a puppy. Then she headed to the window.

She didn't like how high up she was, but the view of the skyscrapers and buildings below was breathtaking. Then she noticed what had gotten her up. It wasn't Jacque's tray; it was the smell of bacon and eggs. All the food at Toni's was pure heaven.

Toni had been so nice to her. He had such a gentle heart. That made him very attractive. Not his features so much. He was a bit overweight, and his beard and eyebrows were a bit too bushy. But it wasn't about looks. It was his smile, his lovely accent, his energy and, more so, his heart. For the first time since they had met, so many years ago, she considered that she could love him. Yes, she could do that.

She stood over the silver tray. Jacque had carefully arranged lovely garnishes around two open porcelain egg jars with coddled eggs. The porcelains were intricately decorated with drawings of two children playing, a boy and a girl. And beside the jars were three strips of bacon and two biscuits.

"You're going to spoil me rotten, Toni." She giggled in delight.

The tray had been placed next to the bed, and there was even a bed tray latched to the side of the cart. Mina didn't use that. She grabbed one of the jars, still hot, and jumped back on the heavenly mattress, staring out at the view. Then she ate her eggs. Of course the eggs were exquisite.

After breakfast, she considered getting dressed, but the lull of the room's comforts, the soft bed, and the silence made her lean back on her side and close her eyes. But she didn't sleep. She kept opening and closing them.

She lay facing the yellow wallpaper. It was darker, almost the color of brass, at night, but now that the sun shone through the window, it was like a bright lemon. She stared at it. It almost tasted sour along her tongue. She peered at all the thin white lines of intricate patterns that looked like webs. The patterns reminded her of the white webbed patterns over the scarlet carpet of the theater. Her eyes grew heavy and she saw that some of the lines overlapped, creating 3D images.

Doing nothing. Maybe this is the quiet I need, Toni. I could do this all day.

In a dreamy state, perhaps asleep, she imagined one of the lines shaped like a wrinkled old man. The upside-down cone-like head had sunken eyes, a warty, pointy nose, and a large toothless grin. Beside the face was a balloon—a yellow balloon, of course—that floated beside the old geezer, on a string, in the wind. And next to that was a stairwell into some sort of circular tunnel.

She refocused her eyes on the stairs. The wall's strange figures seemed to fade back into lines. Replacing them was a vertical uneven crevice, fading in and out, where she had imagined the steps. She might have drifted off for a little bit. Now she blinked her eyes again, trying to make out the figure of the old man. He was gone.

Then she furrowed her brow at the strangest sight. Where she had seen a blurry crevice in the wall, within an arm's distance, there seemed to be a small gap. She reached out to touch the opening in the wall, laughing at herself for being stupid and daydreaming. But then she lost her smile as she watched her hand pass right through.

She snatched her hand back. She jumped up in bed, but she couldn't tear her eyes away from the wall. Slowly, she took her covers off and stood in the small space between the bed and the wall. She ran her hand along the wall again. And once more, her hand passed through a crack. Not only that, now that she was closer, she was able to reach her entire arm inside. It passed through and vanished behind the wall.

Oh, Mina, you're asleep, dreaming … or you're crazy.

She turned back and looked at the room. She saw the tray beside the closed door, the stunning view of Manhattan, and Toni's huge bed. The same lovely bedroom.

She walked through the wall.

She entered a tunnel that descended into an earthen chamber. The dirt walls were glowing the same saffron as the wallpaper. She looked down and saw that she still wore her white camisole and underwear. She pinched her arm, remembering what Erik had done before her adventure at the club. But she didn't wake up in bed.

Her legs moved her toward a brighter light ahead. She squinted then closed her eyes, hoping to open them back in bed. The floor was a little rough, dirty, and cold under her bare feet. Her eyes adjusted to the light, and she found herself at the end of the hall, where the passageway led to a cliff ledge. Below the ledge was a deep chasm surrounded by earthen walls. A valley. The very bottom seemed to move. A thousand snakes slithered under her … no, they were human forms. Muddy, filthy, nude bodies, with their faces dripping tar in that strange blackness again, embracing, kissing, or hugging, and making love with one another. Toward the center was a single concrete pedestal of equal footing to her ledge. It seemed artificial, maybe plastic, in the earthen cave. And upon the concrete platform sat a man—a naked man with legs dangling over the ledge across from her. He was strong with broad shoulders, muscular arms and legs, and ripples along his stomach. And he wore a black ceramic mask and was staring at her with bright-green eyes.

"Where am I, Erik? Is this another dream?"

"Not a dream, mademoiselle," he said, waving a finger. "Real. Your empathic powers call me. Just as we danced in the club. Not a vision, Christine. Real. A real place."

He vanished from the ledge. Then she jumped as she felt fingers run along her cheek. He grasped her shoulder and held her, gesturing to the vast valley below. She tried to escape his grasp, but he locked her in his arms.

"What do you see? Tell me. Lust. Do you see it? Don Juan y Don Juanita? I live an eternity watching all the women and men fuck. Not in fantasy, Christine, but *my* reality. My pleasure." He turned her face, only his mask shading those jade eyes.

She looked down at his naked body.

He followed her glance and smiled. Then he wagged a finger. "But you haven't been guiltless either, have you? Gail. Now Toni. Many more. Love? Or is it lust, Ms. Daaé?"

"What I do is my business."

"Look again," he said, gesturing below. "We are all the same behind the mask. All bodies are a pit of vipers, slithering and sucking. You are Christine, Don Juanita. I am Erik, Don Juan triumphant. None of us ever changes. Neither time nor place alters the base nature of what we truly are. So many bodies below. Come join us and we shall bask in pleasure."

"To die?" she asked, turning from his hungry gaze, furrowing her brow at the bizarre pit below. She tried once more to escape his grasp but she couldn't.

"No," he replied. "Not die. To return to the garden of pleasure."

"Take me away from here," she said, turning her head

from him. "Please, Erik. If you truly care for me. What do you want? Why do you keep tormenting me?"

"You visited him. Now I want you to visit me. Here." He smiled as he spoke, his demeanor oddly docile. "With your voice and my fury, I shall show myself one last time to your audience. For them, faker, I shall appear only once. Behold, that will be enough. When they see me one last time on stage opening night, I shall take you down, down with me. Down here. Here we may stay for all eternity."

And he gestured once more.

"But why? All I want is for you to leave me alone." She closed her eyes. "Please let go of me."

"But I am here," he whispered in her ear. "You cannot escape. No matter where you hide, harlequin, you cannot escape. On your opening night, you shall reveal yourself, faker: wear the makeup, don the mask, climb to your pedestal, and fall. You will do this because you and I are the same. As much as you want to turn from me, from my features, one day you shall don your own black mask. Do not judge me, devil, for I am you. You, too, should hide your face from what you have done to bring about your fall. To every man, every cunt, every soul that you presumed to love, as they bear witness to the pit of your fall, you viper, you faker, you harlequin, you fuck-clown."

"Are you done with the tray, madam?" Jacque's voice seemed shrill and made her jump.

She opened her eyes and awoke with a start in Toni's bed.

She turned and just quietly nodded. He collected it, bowed, and wheeled it out. She turned back to the wall and saw a large, dark, earthen tunnel. And then it was gone, revealing only the yellow wallpaper.

THE NIGHT

After rehearsing for months, it was very hard for Mina to realize that tonight, right now, was *the night*. The night of *The Harlequin*. Not being in the first act, she looked out from the shadows beside the stage to watch her friends dance or sing.

The acrobat she had befriended, Trist, jumped as much as she twirled, doing amazing contortionist acrobatics, bending her body in half and moving about on her hands. Trist had been in a Cirque du Soleil performance for many years. It had enabled her to work with a bunch of bent white rods that she had fashioned around her body. Wearing white tights and in clown face, she gave a performance that was unique and very strange—very *"Toni."*

Then there were the two strong men—giant men, really—who pushed a cart of five short men to a fire truck that was on fire. And a juggler who juggled with fire beside a fake conflagration. And the tightrope, taken out for the first time before her final number, with four tightrope walkers climbing on top of each other. That made Mina laugh when she thought of her own fears of just singing up on the ledge.

"You better go finish up, Mina," said Henson, gently

tapping her shoulder with a smile. "You're up in only another fifteen minutes."

Mina nodded.

"I'm so proud of you," he added. "You're gonna be fantastic."

But she must have looked nervous. Why else would he say that?

Mina tore her eyes away from Toni's circus. His *real* circus. Toni had told her that Act I was really his "macaroni and cheese." The only thing elegant, as of yet, was the orchestra playing Mozart in the background. The rest of the circus was the same as five years before in France.

After Mina changed into her ridiculous heavy gilded scarlet dress and used the restroom in her dressing room a couple of times, she walked to backstage, stage left, and waited painfully as twenty people behind her either stood readying themselves to walk out carrying her tail or inspected the gigantic gauche thing over her shoulder to make sure it was ready for her grand entrance.

As Mina fought with her body, which wanted to use the restroom, yet again, Toni came around backstage with a huge grin. He wore a blue tux, looking out of place among all the circus performers around Mina.

"You make me so happy." He kissed her cheek. "Don't be nervous."

"Why does everyone think I'm nervous?" she asked with an anxious chuckle.

"I've known you for years. And recently, at our home, we've become far closer."

She nodded.

"As usual," he added, "you're less sure of yourself than everyone else."

"I'm not."

"Mina, can you turn to the left," said a stagehand readjusting her costume. "I need to clasp this."

"Good luck." And he hugged her. "You'll do great. I know it."

She turned and felt like a hundred pounds had been added to her left shoulder. *At least he didn't say break a leg.*

Oh, but I am nervous, Toni. I think I'm going to die if they don't let me on stage now.

Why is it always easier once I'm on stage? Just standing here is driving me crazy.

"One more minute, Ms. Daaé."

He had to say that. Like after doing this a thousand times, I don't know my cue to walk on stage?

By now, Toni had masterfully introduced the eighteenth century into the Big Top, and two colonial women in long coats with hoods and hand muffs were singing opera on one side of the stage while a bunch of foolish clowns were juggling or sauntering aimlessly on the other side.

She heard the familiar start of Mozart's Mass in C Minor K. 427 matched with the moving choral of the two singers in colonial attire on stage. Toni's work had masterfully shifted the mood of ridiculousness to a somber note, Mozart's piece asking us to weep for God's mercy in the midst of fools. It was time for Mina's grand entrance. Why had Toni chosen this piece to introduce her? And why was she thinking of that now? But she was. Mina stepped slowly on stage, with twenty people following her, amid gasps from the audience. Jesters stopped juggling to stare at the red serpent walking onstage, and everyone stopped to look at her. Her. How could they not? Her form took up the entire stage.

And then she sang with the most beautiful voice she could muster. And this was it. She was singing on Broadway. She was actually singing on Broadway! And Toni planned the production in such a way that every head in the auditorium—there were over a thousand people in the audience—and every eye looked upon her. She sang "Kyrie Eleison": "Lord have mercy on us." Other voices sang with her.

Stealing from Mozart? Perhaps. But typical of her new

lover, Toni also knew the history behind this piece. He smoothly transitioned the orchestral music to "Et Incarnatus Est." When Mozart had first performed this song in Strasbourg, this had been sung by his new wife, Constanze. Coincidence? Doubtful. Toni rarely acted without purpose in his art. Had he planned this for his "new wife"? His new lover?

Whatever the case, Mina sang the piece, happily filling the role. She sang it not only for the play but in celebration of him. And this was easy because she loved him. She sang it with all her soul for him, not only because she wanted to be what the audience aspired for her to be but because she adored the music and the man who had brought it to them.

When it was over, all the lights dimmed, and Mina and her crew left the dark stage. The applause shook the walls and ceiling of the theater as she was crowded backstage with all her helpers.

"Incredible, Mina!" cried Henson.

Daniella placed a hand on her. "Nicely done."

Then they removed the heavy tail. Henson ran to other performers to get ready for the finishing acts. Mina looked around for Toni, but he wasn't there.

"Get in your dance clothes now," said Daniella with her usual smugness. "If you actually move as well as you sing, we might just have the success Toni thinks we'll have."

Mina felt on top of the world in her dressing room. She'd had accolades before but never for an actual performance. She could do this. She knew that now. She could actually make *The Harlequin* a success. She could be a star.

Quickly, she grabbed her white tights and pulled them on. Then she ran to her chair and looked at her face under the bright lights around her vanity mirror. Her face was already powdered white, and there was a hint of red along her nose matching the red on her lips. She carefully ran her hand along the side of her hair, straightening a few curls.

"A wonderful performance, Christine."

"Who's there!" Mina whirled around but saw no one in her dressing room.

She searched the room. Then she faced the mirror. To her horror, a man wearing a Pierrot clown face and white tights just like hers, but with a black mask over his eyes, sat on a stool across the room in the shadows. Mina turned again and he was gone.

"I'm here," he said with a laugh.

She recognized his French accent.

Mina turned back and saw him again in the mirror. This time he was standing, wearing a black cloak and long black cape with his black mask.

"Before I unveil myself to your audience, mademoiselle, I would like to congratulate you. Whatever happens in this fucking freak show, I wanted you to know that you did spectacularly. You sang much better than I ever did. Much better than anyone ever did in your role. Of course the words were Herr Mozart, yes? I take it Toni's message wasn't for me, his long-lost love? Perhaps for Herr Mozart's Constanze? Or if not Constanze, then perhaps Christine … for Toni's Christine Daaé?"

"You're not here, Erik," she said, shaking her head. "I'm not seeing you."

"You're not. I'm in the mirror."

"Leave me alone," she pleaded, looking down at the carpet, avoiding the mirror. "If you care for me, Erik, please leave. This is our opening night."

"Now don't upset me." He sounded angry.

She could see his reflection leaning forward and wagging a finger at her.

"The one thing I couldn't do after I fell is what you do next. *Dance.* Don't do that. But you are, aren't you? You are going to try to dance, aren't you? And you know what? You might be a fine singer, bitch, but your cavorting is an embarrassment. It's rather like the way you make love."

"Please, stop. Shut up." And she put her hands to her ears. "Just stop saying anything."

And there was silence. Mina slowly pulled her hands away, and she jumped at the sight of Erik still standing behind her in the mirror. She felt his hand run down her arm. Now he wore white tights with a painted frown behind his mask, exactly as Mina would be dressed for her dance performance in Act II. Mina turned to face him, but he was gone.

"Stop it! God, please stop it, Erik!"

"This shall be the last time I need to show myself," said his voice. "Don't worry. You will see me with everyone when you fall. Your fall shall be glorious. Glory be to you, not God. Such a fall will be in the papers and you will be famous… Ah, but I age myself. What do you use for news nowadays? When you fall, ma chérie, we can be together in pleasure, like I showed you, for an eternity."

Mina got up and straightened her tights. She looked in her mirror, satisfied with her appearance. Erik, still on the periphery, staring at her body, seemed satisfied too.

"You can only pretend I'm not here for so long."

Mina reached over to her purse on the table. She opened it and looked at a medicine bottle, thinking of taking some pills, but she feared they would make her drowsy during her performance.

"And that," he whispered near her ear, "won't get rid of me either."

Mina closed her eyes. "If you love me, Erik, you won't ruin the show. Please. Don't mess this up for me. This is everything to me."

"Everything to you or everything to your fuck-clown? Oh, sweet Ms. Daaé, but it was everything to *me*." He flashed a slithery, sardonic smile. "And who ever said I love you?"

There was a knock on the door.

"Come in!" Mina snapped more loudly than she intended.

Toni walked in with his grand smile.

Erik flashed the nastiest scowl in the mirror but then disappeared.

"Wonderful, Mina! Absolutely wonderful!" He ran over and hugged her. Then he moved her back a little, searching her face. "What's the matter? You look upset."

"God, Toni. I saw him again."

Toni furrowed his brow. Then he lost his smile. "Not now, Mina. Please." His voice was not kind. It was angry.

Mina simply nodded.

"Save your energy for the finale."

"But he's here, he's really here. He said I'm psychic. I must be bringing him to our opening night because of the stress … Oh, forget it. I'll try to ignore him."

"Just do what you did a minute ago," he said with a sigh. "You stole the show. My God, Mina, we could have just done that one song and the audience would still be at our feet."

"Thanks."

"I'm so proud of you." He kissed her on the lips.

As he did, she could have sworn she saw the reflection of a man in a mask, in the mirror, glaring at them.

"Dance like the wind, Mina," he said quietly. "Sing like an angel. If you do that, this show will be a smash. I know it."

"I know, Toni. I know." Then she forced a smile. "Of course, you know my song was sung by Constanze."

"Che? Constanze? Do not honor me so, my dear," he said with a laugh, putting a hand on her shoulder. "I am not Herr Mozart."

"But I do love you, Toni." She looked up into his eyes. "I do. You've cared about me more than anyone ever has. I sang the piece for you, Toni. I love you."

"I love you too, Mina." He hugged her tightly. "Now, best of luck." He kissed her cheek and whispered, "I love you so much."

CRACK.

They both jumped and turned toward the wall of vanity mirrors. A large line had appeared across a mirror.

ACT II

Don Giovanni opens with Don Giovanni wooing and
raping a woman, then killing the father of the woman he
ravaged. Not so in *The Harlequin*. There was no death. If there
was any figure of foreboding, it was the mix of grandeur and
power exuded by Mina's introduction. No. There was no
murder or violence in Toni's play. But there were suitors.
Loads of them. And clowns. Lots of them too. And there was
Mina Daaé. Mina was what Act II was really about.

After her triumphant entrance, she sat nervously backstage in her white leotard. A pianist played Liszt in the
orchestra pit. Then she had her cue, a bit of rouge was
brushed on her white-painted cheeks, and she rushed back to
center stage.

Male ballet dancers with much thicker white face paint
rushed around her. Some pushed each other, others pulled
away. All the while, Mina stood frozen. She didn't dance. She
was more like a white prop on stage. She was not as grand,
but as she was the only dancer not moving, the audience's eyes
fell upon her.

Finally, when surrounded by ten of them, she pushed the
men from her with a broad, theatrical stroke of her arms.

One allowed space for her to twirl and she did her best. She even heard a bit of applause, likely from someone already enamored with her performance in the red dress. Then she did a few leaps and turns, not a stellar grand jeté or glissade—hardly good enough for Daniella, and barely suitable for Broadway—but enough to mark her territory as a dancer. Then came two men. One took her hand and twirled with her as the lights shone over them. He led her, moving her fast to the rhythm of the ebony and ivory playing like waves in the sea, until another ballet dancer in clown face grabbed her other arm. The two spun around her, and the dance became a bizarre competition, vying for her attention.

She took the role of bystander once more. One suitor was knocked down. Mina ran to the fallen man and helped him up. As she lifted him, she raised her head to the other dancer and shamed him by dancing with the fallen man. And so it went on.

Soon came women. They, too, swarmed the stage, twirling and dancing a wonderful waltz with some of the men. And once more a suitor came to take Mina's hand. This time a woman.

Mina had never liked watching female dancers. Their movements were more fluid than hers, reminding her painfully of her failures. But she tried. She danced. The play went on and on like this, with an occasional fool from the Big Top rushing on stage and being splashed by water or stumbling.

Everything went as rehearsed until an unusual suitor in a long, black cape walked onstage. A performer Mina did not recognize. One who wore a shiny black mask and black cape over his leotard. As he took her hand, he said in her ear, "My dear Christine, how are you going to pretend that I'm not here now?"

"I told you to stop, Erik," she hissed by his ear as he raised her hand over her head. She wasn't miked, so she didn't need to worry about the audience hearing them. "Not now!"

He didn't stop. He threw his cape on the stage and, in his white leotard and mask, he danced, following the correct steps for the play.

"Embarrassing pas de bourrée, mon ami," he said beside her. "No, no, no. This will not do. Je n'aime pas ça! Allow me to show you how to dance."

And he stopped, released her hand, and stomped on the ground. Many of the other dancers fled the stage. Then, alone, Erik twirled to center stage as Mina stood and watched. Other dancers gasped as this was not a part of their regular routine. Mina froze. Then Erik did what Toni had said only he could do. He danced as if he were skipping water, or skating, with elegance Mina had never seen before. All the dancers and actors on stage froze, watching him. Many people backstage were staring too. When there were enough sounds coming from the audience, he bowed broadly before Mina and reached out his hand for her.

Mina just stood in shock.

"Move!" Henson said in a forced whisper from backstage. "Mina, dance! Dance!"

She took his hand and they returned to a waltz; this time, Mina was having a difficult time keeping up with her feet. He twirled her around as if she were a prop.

"Erik, you have to slow down. I can't keep up with you."

"I thought I wasn't real?" And he swung Mina right up against his body, his face close enough to kiss her. And then he did. He kissed her with more violence than romance. The audience cheered.

"Why are you here?" Mina asked.

"I'm here to witness your fall," he whispered in her ear, grasping her close. "I've already told you that. Many times."

They held each other. Mina barely noticed their movements, but she was moving. He was lifting her entire body with great strength, and she was simply gliding on her toes.

"But why, Erik? If you care about me? I don't want to go with you. I want—"

"To be with Toni?"

He leaned her down close to the ground, and she could clearly see a scowl through the opening in his black mask. The movements were similar to those in their rehearsal, but far more violent. The audience had no clue, but Mina guessed the producers were going crazy watching the two of them dance off cue.

"Erik, I love him."

"Christine loved Raoul once. Erik didn't grace you with his feet then. Your mind allows this. Your psychic power. Your empathic energy, almost as magical and wondrous as your voice. Christine, you are an angel, but you shall be my fallen angel. Like Don Giovanni, you are a lascivious whore. Your punishment for your lovers shall be your fall. First Gail, now you. That is why we dance. 'Tis a funeral dance. A requiem in celebration of your fall. Relish the splendor!"

"Toni hasn't taken me," Mina said, shaking her head between spins. She came close to his face, but the spin made her dizzy.

Under the mask, he squinted his glowing jade eyes in the darkness and shook his head.

"I'm not taken."

She skipped a step and nearly fell, but Erik caught her. Then he spun her like a top. She felt like his prop, his fan or poi. He was so good that she only had to do her best to move her feet with him.

"I'm not talking about you, stupide bitch! I care nothing for you! You've taken my love. My life. I love Toni. And just like Christine, you shall fall."

Before she could respond, he spun her again. Her feet dragged in circles over the wooden floor, and he let her go. Such was the centripetal force that the whole theater spun around her with the purple light on the ceiling swirling. She heard gasps from the audience. And, for a flash, she saw a bright light shine over one of the top balconies at the back of the theater. There, under the fifth balcony, illuminated by a floodlight above the packed theater, was the naked body of Gail dangling from a rope. Gail was swaying and turning.

"Putain!" Erik violently grabbed her in his arms. Then he pointed up at the balcony and snapped, "Look. Look now! You killed her. Feel love? See what it did to her, poor girl. She took her life, but she died from your rejection. Because of you. Now I reject you! I love Monsieur Vollini. So decide. What shall be your fate, Christine? Rope or ledge?"

The lights were cut. It became pitch black and Erik let Mina go. She fell out of his arms and spun in circles onto the ground in darkness. The applause raged so loudly in the auditorium that it hurt her ears.

When Mina did not get up, people from backstage rushed to help her. She was half carried offstage.

"Incredible!" Daniella exclaimed to Mina. "I don't believe it!"

Mina blinked and caught Daniella's face looking down at her with the strangest thing she had ever seen—a smile.

"I've never seen you move like that." Daniella was still weirdly grinning.

"Get her a bag," said Vince, crouching over her. "She's not well. Something to breathe in. Quick. She's hyperventilating. She fainted, Dani."

"Well, I couldn't expect any better," Daniella replied with a shrug. "I don't think I've ever seen anyone dance like that."

Mina nodded, snatched a bag from a dancer, and breathed deeply inside it. "Can't … breathe." She looked up at Dani as a few dancers helped her up from the floor and onto a chair. "Glad … you liked it," she said, breathing through the bag.

"Liked it?" Daniella shook her head. "Are you kidding? I loved it."

"Great job, Mina!" cried another stagehand, touching her shoulder.

The audience thundered with applause in the dark auditorium, and they wouldn't stop.

"Great job," shouted a dancer in black tights walking by her.

"Incredible," said another.

"*Give her space!*" snapped Henson. "Back away." And they obeyed their director. "Are you okay, Mina? What happened?"

Mina breathed deeply into the plastic bag again. "Where's Toni?"

"We've got another emergency with the lighting," said Henson, running a hand through his thin hair. "I don't know if you happened to notice, but the light shone on one of the balconies. It's always something. But how are you? Are you all right?"

She just nodded.

"You finally saw him," Mina said.

Daniella furrowed her brow. Then she turned to Henson, who also looked confused.

"You finally saw Erik, didn't you? Good. I … I think I finally understand why he's been haunting me. He loves Toni. He doesn't love me. See, Toni loved Erik. Now he's here for revenge over Toni's love for me. He wants to ruin the play because Toni loves me now. And ruin me. He intends to kill me in the last act."

"What's she talking about?" asked Vince.

"Did you take your medicine?" Daniella asked.

"Erik … didn't you see him, Vince?" Mina asked.

Vince shook his head.

She looked up at twenty faces, now hovering over her. Most were just patting her shoulder or waving a jovial thumbs-up.

But a few looked at her like she wasn't well. That gave her the familiar sinking feeling again.

"But … didn't you all see him? He was incredible. He was so graceful. He danced as if he were on ice. Just like Toni said he would. But … I understand now. I get why the phantom is haunting me. See, it's Toni. He loves Toni, not me. He doesn't care about me. It's all Toni."

"Fantastic, Mina!" Toni crouched down by the chair and touched her shoulder. "Incredible." He turned to Daniella. "I told you."

Daniella permitted a nod, but she was finally starting to lose her smile and look like her old bitchy self again.

"If you can't go on, Mina, we'll stop the show," Vince said.

"Che?" asked Toni. "What did he just say? Can't go on? Stop the show?"

But he wasn't the only one staring at Vince. All heads, including members of the stage crew, some actors in colonial clothes, and some dancers, turned and stared at Vince.

"She's not well," explained Vince. "She looks pale. She fainted after the dance."

"She's wearing clown makeup," Henson remarked.

Toni said quietly, "Mina, what is it? Are you okay?"

"I don't know if I should do the last act. Erik wants to kill me. He wants me to fall just like he did. I don't know if I can go up there."

"I thought we were through this," Toni said. "I won't let anything bad happen to you."

"It's not up to you." Mina shook her head violently. But then she looked deep into his eyes. She thought of his play. She'd rather die than stop his play. She took another deep breath in the bag and nodded.

"Mina," Toni said, grabbing her hand. "I'll be up there if anything happens."

But she wasn't worried Toni wouldn't be there. She was worried the phantom would be there.

"That was fantastic, Mina!" cried a stagehand, tapping her shoulder.

"Just give her some space!" snapped Henson.

"Great job, Mina," interrupted another dancer. She was with two extras and they all nodded excitedly, each putting a hand on her shoulder.

But then one asked, cocking his head back as they walked away, "Is she all right?"

"It must be the stress of opening night," Vince said. Then he forced a smile at Mina. "It wouldn't be the first time a performer fainted. All I know is your dance was amazing. It was one of the best performances I've ever seen. It wasn't all scripted but, why not? Who cares? The way you moved. I don't think Daniella thought you could even do those moves."

"I didn't," Daniella admitted.

Vince had asked if they should stop the show. Was he kidding? Everyone had looked at him like he was crazy. Even Mina. She could never do that, especially not with the joyous look now splashed on Toni's face. He was so excited. Even if the critics and the audience hated the show, he'd be overjoyed that his dream had come true.

She took a deep breath into her bag again and looked up at all of them once more. "But did you see the man with the mask dancing with me? He was…"

They hadn't.

"Toni, he said he's going to make me fall to the stage after the net's cut."

"I won't allow it," Toni said, grabbing her hand. "No, I won't. Even if you fall, you'll have the safety wire. And not only that, I'll be up there right with you."

Mina nodded and tried to force a smile.

"Are they practicing?" Daniella asked Henson.

Henson just shrugged.

DON GIOVANNI

Mina sat backstage, stage right, on a stool, watching clowns fight one another in a circus scene as a makeup artist wiped the clown makeup from her face. Toni had said he wouldn't have her in clown face in the final act. Her black hair flowed around her now-naked face. Then the artist applied makeup just to accentuate her natural facial features. Meanwhile, others helped throw the heavy, flabby white clown outfit over her shoulders and fasten the wire to it. Another stagehand slipped on the ridiculous large red clown shoes. She had to get ready quickly. Her suitors, more clowns, were already fighting with one another—some actually fighting, others simply dancing—waiting for the Harlequin to arrive.

The fighting stopped. Then she saw what she dreaded. Stagehands in dark camouflage slowly rolled the giant two-tower structure to the back of the stage as the chaos continued up front. Mina knew it came with a tightrope this time, but the tower stood so high that she couldn't see it.

"You're doing amazing," said the makeup artist.

"Thanks, Carl."

Carl was the key makeup artist, an effeminate gay man who Mina loved. He was so sweet. "Gosh, Mina, I don't know how you do this next scene," he said, looking up at the towers. "It's so high up there. I hate heights."

"I don't like heights either," Mina said. "Just don't tell anyone."

"Keep doing what you're doing," he said with a laugh. "You're amazing." Then he saw a cue from someone closer to the stage. "None of the dancers ever danced like that." He brushed her nose and part of her cheek. "That's it. You're up."

Mina had difficulty swallowing. She lifted the legs of her ridiculous frilly outfit; it was so heavy and unwieldy. Then she made her way to the ladder by the steel tower.

Carl stopped her, grabbing her shoulder. "Mina, don't forget the cape."

"Oh, can you help me put it on?"

Carl fastened the black cape over her flabby white suit for her finale. It was hot in all the clothes. Though they were not nearly as stifling as her red dragon dress, now she had to climb the ladder carrying all of it.

"Good luck!" Carl said with a big smile, and he lightly pushed her back from behind.

She walked to the ladder.

In the darkness at the back of the stage, few people could see her. Some actresses by the stage tapped her arm and whispered, "Good luck." The whole time, looking back, she was blinded by the bright lights shining on the stage. And laughter. Clowns were doing the most ridiculous things before she went on.

She touched the metal ladder of the pedestal. It was cold. A few stagehands rushed from behind to help lift her baggy clothes over the first step. Then she started climbing alone.

As she climbed, she heard the orchestra prepare. It was a prelude before *Don Giovanni*, the overture. But in the middle of it all was a distant cacophony of saxophones and drums. Between the fools and the noise, it was madness, something Toni was very good at creating.

Her hands shook. They always shook as she climbed the ladder, but tonight it was far worse. Not only was it opening night; it was the night of her "fall," according to her devil.

Just one step at a time. You can do this. One step. Then another.

He's real. Erik was real. He must be. Though she might be able to squeak by as a dancer on Broadway, her glorious choreographic performance tonight had not been her own. It had been too perfect. He had moved her. Perhaps he would make her fall now. After all, the net was stretched below the pedestal, not the ladder. And she felt his breath beside her. Somehow, she *felt* him. And then she heard him.

"You're really going through with this," Erik whispered by her ear. "Despite all my warnings?"

"I thought you wanted me to fall?" Again, she wasn't miked. She knew that her microphone would only turn on when *Don Giovanni* started thundering.

"It's inevitable. But it really isn't about you."

"You're jealous. You want me to die because I'm in love with Toni?" Her hatred of him, her anger, pushed her legs to climb the steps faster.

"No. I want you to die because he's in love with you. Your fall is glorious vengeance for what he did to me. A fitting revenge. Makes perfect sense, Christine, no?"

"Liar. The only Christine was my great-ancestor in Paris. My name is Mina. Devil, watch me fall. Let it happen. I don't care. It will be the greatest finale. Our show shall be the greatest show on Broadway."

"The greatest show? Indeed. Only ... I'm afraid to tell you this, *Mina*, but the net is not the only thing cut. I loosened your wire from the fly tower."

Her legs weakened from those words, but she didn't stop climbing. She did slow a little, though. And yet, even despite this final threat, she made it to the top. She didn't dare look down. Slowly, with her body still shaking, she climbed onto the parapet.

The orchestra thundered. There was no longer time to

think. The platform shook. The violins and drums thundered, and she knew that her microphone was now operational. She was surrounded by purple light. A violet floodlight filled the pedestal.

"Don Giovanni …" Her voice rang out strongly in the strange tenor sung by a woman. She was supposed to stand, but she was afraid. This being the first show, half of her involuntarily pushed herself up on her knees, but feeling that particular unpleasant rise in her butt, she couldn't stand as rehearsed. Yet she sang on. She just sat on her knees as her voice rang out her accusations to the theater below. Meanwhile, lights shone on clowns onstage surrounding her, looking up, and pointing at her. They sang the words of Don Giovanni as she played the part of their accuser: the Commendatore.

She forced herself to stand. Then she swept her arm down toward the stage in a broad, threatening gesture, staring with wide-open eyes, accusing all of them. She pointed at the clowns on stage, then the clowns off center stage, and then the crowd, every single one of them, the entire amphitheater guilty of sinful lust and disgrace.

There was no net. She could see that now. There was no net between her and the cold wooden floor. But she didn't stop singing. This was her moment. The moment of her theatrical triumph. And she sang her part as the statue, the judge, and the accuser judging them all.

Yet her triumph was shaken as a light switched on over a balcony, the fifth balcony again. Once more, she saw her best friend dangling from a rope. Gail was more real, more terrible, wearing her fuchsia coat and jeans, her long blonde hair and tranquil closed eyes spotlighted, shifting ever so slightly over the audience. Then the light shut off and Gail disappeared.

Replacing it was another purple floodlight shining on the pedestal across from her. Erik, adorned in his black mask and cape, wearing the same baggy white clown outfit underneath, like her own, accompanied her in a familiar baritone, just as he had done in the audition.

That's when there was a disturbance on stage. Many clowns moved back and stared as a man in a blue tuxedo rushed frantically across the stage. Floodlights shone over him. It was Toni. He was waving his hands desperately at the orchestra for them to stop. But the orchestra played and Mina kept singing.

At the bottom of her ladder, Toni shouted, "She can't jump! The net's cut! She must get down from the ladder! Get her down now!" His words competed with the loud orchestra and her voice, but more lights turned on across the stage. "Get down, Mina! It's not safe. Don't do the final jump!" he cried, looking up at her. Some in the audience stood up in a panic. "Stop the play!" But the orchestra played on. "My God, stop the music!" Toni kept shouting, but it was difficult to hear him. He wasn't miked.

He rushed to the ladder and started to climb.

Mina didn't stop singing. And the orchestra kept playing. All the performers ignored Toni and resumed the opera. Then Mina pointed down at him, wide-eyed once more under the violet light, accusing her lover below.

Every light in the theater turned on.

"Come down, Mina! The net's cut."

From a glance at her periphery, she saw many in the audience stand by their seats. She could see their faces more clearly now, over a thousand, as they stared up at her, some with hands covering their mouths, others signaling for her to go down the ladder. At first, she trembled seeing all of them, so far below, watching her. Then she stood taller, gazing down and accusing all of them, her voice ringing out more strongly than ever.

She saw the phantom, in her periphery, walk across the tightrope. When he was close enough, he started to pull at her arm, back and forth, trying to push her off the parapet. Mina heard screams as she teetered for a moment over the edge.

Then, on her other side, Toni appeared at the top of the ledge, grasping for her hand.

"Verrai (You come)," Mina sang.

Toni pleaded for her to take his hand. His eyes looked deep into hers, and she could feel his love. His care moved her so much that she nearly broke character. It was as real to her as her phantom now tugging her other arm. But then she remembered her role as Commendatore. The play would have its fall. She opened her eyes wide and pointed at Toni once more.

"Dammi la mano in pegno (Give me thy hand in token)," Mina sang.

"Eccola (Here)!" Toni cried, reaching again for her to take his hand.

A security guard rushed across the stage and stood under the ladder. "Don't fall! The net is cut!"

"Cos'hai (What's wrong)?" sang Mina, looking down at the guard under the ladder.

The crowd panicked, with many onlookers rushing to the front rows of the auditorium, shouting for Mina to climb down.

Then Toni grabbed her arm to pull her onto the ladder, but Erik snatched her wrist over the tightrope. Mina marveled that Erik could pull her at all while remaining balanced. They tugged her back and forth. Finally, Mina freed her arms from both of them, nearly falling off the ladder. Many in the audience gasped, trying to climb onto the stage.

"*My God, help her down!*" cried a woman's voice.

"Pentiti (Repent)!" Mina cried to Toni.

"No!" Toni said.

"Pentiti!"

"No."

"Si."

"No."

"Si."

"No."

"Sì"

"No! No!"

"Ah! Tempo più non v'è (There is no more time)!"

It was her time. Her time on Broadway!

And here is where I soar.

Toni reached out for her once more.

She gazed down at his hand and then the glove of the Phantom. Their reaching hands reminded her of her painting. That painting was still on the easel by her bed. The image somehow gave her comfort in her lonely apartment. She had slept with that hand in darkness, knowing it always reached for her as she slept, just as Toni was reaching for her now. But in the painting, it had been her creation. Now it was Toni and an apparition.

"Tutto a tue colpe é poco (This is nothing, compared to your sins)," sang voices from the auditorium. "Vieni, c'è un mal peggior (Come, there is a worse pain)!"

"Mina!" Toni shouted so loud that his voice echoed in the theater despite not being miked, competing with the music by the orchestra. "Forget the play! Stop the singing and come down. Please! Don't do this!" Toni's eyes were tearing as he desperately reached out for her again.

She stared at his hand once more, gazing at his naked fingers. Each finger a part of a machine that reached out to her like the hand dripping paint on her canvas. How could this muscle, bone, and sinew be of such importance to her? To anyone?

"Tutto a tue colpe é poco (This is nothing, compared to your sins). Vieni, c'è un mal peggior (Come, there is a worse pain)!"

Of far greater elegance was Erik's glove. Even now, as the phantom was attempting to throw her from the precipice, he brushed her fingers with the lovely softness of his glove.

"I don't care about the play!" Toni shouted, violently shaking his head. "I don't. I don't care about it."

Mina looked into Toni's eyes and nodded.

"Take my hand. I only care about you, Mina. *I love you!*"

"Che inferno, che terror (What a hell, what a terror)!"

That was her theatrical cue. She grabbed Toni's hand while yanking her other hand from Erik. The phantom shifted uneasily on the rope by her side. Then he let out a scream heard through the speakers. She watched the fiend fall.

He fell like a sack from the ceiling rafters and pounded the wooden stage below. There was a rush of screams and gasps from the audience, and anyone still on stage scattered.

All turned dark.

Then a single light fell on a body lying at the center of the stage, wrapped in a black cape. And in that moment no one, not one clown on stage or spectator in the auditorium, moved.

The silence was broken when a clown with thick, curly red hair appeared, stage right, wearing a baggy white outfit and twirling a cane. Theater lighting followed him as he sauntered his way across the stage, over to the fallen body. Then he used his wooden cane to poke and prod. He turned to the audience, then looked down at the fallen body. The phantom's pitch-black cape was wrapped so tightly around the body that it reminded Mina of a burial shroud. The clown grabbed the cape and, like a magician pulling a cloth off a table, yanked it from the body with great bravado. There was nothing underneath. The clown swirled the cape around him and draped it over his shoulders. Then he gave a grand bow before the audience.

There was silence. Complete shock. Then applause. A deafening applause.

"I love you," Mina whispered in Toni's arms, both looking down. "I love you so much."

All the lights dimmed. Then a single light delicately shone over Mina and Toni. They held each other tightly in an embrace and kissed.

"We did it, Mina."

THE MASQUERADE

Mina was nervous. She sat beside Toni before a large table on the brightly lit stage after *The Harlequin*. They wore thick Pierrot clown face and puffy white clown costumes. There were signs everywhere saying No Flash Photography, but that was ignored, and Mina had to keep squinting.

"What's fame like, Ms. Daaé?" asked an older woman with long hair. She was in the front row behind bright lights. Mina's first question. A direct one. And with the rest of the reporters laughing.

"I don't know," she said with a chuckle, looking at Toni. He squeezed her hand. "Not much different from before, I guess."

"But people crowd you. They want your autograph or a picture. Everyone's enamored with you after only one night. It's like instant fame. How do you cope?"

"I help her," said Toni, leaning into the microphone.

They laughed.

"They rush you too, Mr. Vollini. But you two are close, right? There are rumors she's staying at your house. Is that true?"

"Her house."

The reporters laughed.

"So there's something going on between you two? Producer and star?"

"Did you think *The Harlequin* would be such a hit, Toni?" interjected a young male interviewer. He was wearing glasses, but Mina couldn't make out much else behind the bright lights.

"I dreamt it so," Toni said with a nod. "We were very successful in Europe, but that was a different play than in the States. It was more of a circus. Not opera. And we never had success to this degree. Of course, it's mainly because of my star. The musical would have gone nowhere without the voice of Mina Daaé. Her voice touches God."

"Oh, stop," Mina said, hitting his shoulder.

"'Tis true." He looked deeply into her eyes. "If I didn't have you, it would have gone nowhere here."

"So there is something between you two?" asked the woman again.

Toni leaned close to Mina and kissed her on the lips. It was a peck, but the camera flashes went crazy. Mina quickly moved away and shielded her eyes. So did Toni.

Mina knew that this photo was gold. Two clowns sitting together onstage, kissing. It was almost as if they had planned a perfect photo op for a press release. And, knowing Toni, it probably was.

"You played the role in Europe, right?" asked another interviewer. He looked more like a spectator, coming from a row farther back.

"Yeah, yeah. But it wasn't the same. I was trained to sing Herr Mozart, but my voice doesn't touch God like Mina's does."

They laughed but Toni remained quite serious.

"What about—"

"So you two are living together now?" interrupted the woman interviewer. "For the record."

"For the record?" Mina leaned into the microphone. "Yes."

"And the act where—"

"Toni was so kind to give me the role," Mina said. "I didn't expect that." She was surprised to see the whole auditorium quiet down as she spoke. She didn't like the sound of her voice. It sounded a little shaky. She gripped her hand tightly. "I mean, I always wanted to perform … but I never really thought I was good enough. Toni gave me the confidence to stand up here in front of all of you and sing and dance. Performing is a difficult thing, you know. It's like … like being unclothed. Naked. Fragile, breakable. I don't think a lot of people know that. And I'm not trying to be arrogant."

"You could never be arrogant, Ms. Daaé," interjected the woman interviewer.

"Thanks." Then there was more silence as Mina gathered her thoughts. All their eyes were on her. "You really don't know what it's like on stage. I wish you could experience what it's like for me. It's free, but scary. I think that's what Toni is conveying with his ending." Then she put her finger to her chin and said, "There's a power there. A naked, almost primal, power that I feel when I'm showing my raw self and performing before you. It's terrifying, but electrifying. It's free. If I can express that freedom, even for a moment, you know, show the naked raw person behind my mask, then I succeeded in my performance and I'm satisfied. And I get to perform this every night because of Toni. He says he owes the show to me but, no, actually I owe it to him."

"Oh, cara mia," Toni said, rubbing her back, "thank you."

The auditorium became loud. There was a great deal of murmuring, and some of the interviewers talked over each other.

"But really, Toni," Mina added, "I think—" She looked deeply into his eyes.

Toni just smiled sweetly.

"Toni, I think they like your play so much because it's real. I know it's why I do. The pomp is there, the silliness, the clowns, but then it all comes crashing down in the end and becomes real. Very real, you know?"

"Why don't we talk about that last act?" said the interviewer. "At the end, it was terrifying watching you, on opening night, because so many people thought you were actually going to fall, Ms. Daaé. I remember really feeling like you were going to jump. Yes, it was frightening. Just like you said. No one could see your wire. And Toni acted genuinely panicked as he rushed up the ladder. All the lights were on, like now. It was as if the play was over. And Toni wasn't even dressed up in any costume. He just had on the suit for opening night. It was really you two, and there was a desperate sense that it would be over for you, Ms. Daaé—not the show, your life. Yes, it was real. So many of us in the audience were scared."

"I was scared too," Toni said, leaning into the microphone. Many in the audience laughed. "I was. It's a very difficult piece to perform. Many years ago, one of my beloved actors actually fell."

"We've heard that."

"Si …" Toni took a deep breath and Mina touched his arm. "I've had to live through that memory over and over. It's very hard. But the drama was written by him. Don Giovanni and Mozart with the fall were all written by him. So, as difficult as it is to repeat it, in a way, I perform it in honor of his life. And I know he would not want it any other way."

"So you're going to do it every show? What about safety codes, with everyone rushing the stage? And will the stunt even work when people start expecting it?"

"The play will go on as it did opening night," Toni said dismissively. "I will not dishonor my friend's work. We will play out his fall. You can judge it any way you like. The art is our art."

"But there won't be a net? It's seems so unsafe."

"No, I've assured it is absolutely safe for me and Mina." And he squeezed her hand and gave her a sweet smile. "I wrote the play to draw the audience in. And I think you get that. Anyway, if I changed it, it wouldn't be *The Harlequin*."

"But what about you, Mina?" asked the lady behind the lights. "Do you intend to perform the same way? Risking your life? Singing and standing high on a pedestal where there's no safety net below?"

"For sure."

"But you said earlier that you were afraid of heights?"

"The harlequin performed it in Paris," she said with a shrug. "So why not me?"

"I love you, Mina," Toni said.

"I love you, too, Toni."

And the two clowns kissed again. There were a lot of camera flashes. And there was applause.

THE END

READ THE REST OF PHANTOM HEARTS

An angel & ghost romance collection.
Each novel is a distinct standalone story.

- SHADES
- HAUNTING JOY

The books in this series are coming soon on audiobook! Enjoy Phantom Masquerade, narrated by Caitlin Kelly; Haunting Joy and Shades coming soon.

ACKNOWLEDGMENTS

I want to thank my beta readers Monique S. and George B. for running through another manuscript and providing invaluable advice in shaping this novel. And to the polishing of my manuscript by my line editor, Stephanie Ward, and my proofreader, Faith Williams. And to my cover artist Mirella Santana for creating stunning eye-catching artwork.

And finally to the genius of Wolfgang Amadeus Mozart's music and Gaston Leroux's original tale for providing inspiration.

PARTING WORDS

What did you think of *Phantom Masquerade*? By placing a book review, you can inform others of your thoughts and help spread the word about my book.

Want more? Periodically I like to send news regarding current or new projects. If you'd like to be privy, I encourage you to sign up to my email newsletter. Your information will remain private and you can cancel any time.

Sign up at www.alhawke.com or scan the following QR code:

ABOUT THE AUTHOR

A.L. Hawke is the author of the bestselling Hawthorne University Witch series. The author lives in Southern California torching the midnight candle over lovers against a backdrop of machines, nymphs, magic, spice and mayhem. A.L. Hawke writes fantasy and romance spanning four thousand years, from pre-civilization to contemporary and beyond.

Visit A.L. Hawke at www.alhawke.com

Email: contact@alhawke.com